# JUST PLAIN BOB

# Gail's
# PRICE
## ROMANCE EROTICA

# WARNING

This book contains sexually explicit scenes and adult language. It may be considered offensive to some readers. This book is for sale to adults ONLY.

Please store your files wisely where they cannot be accessed by underage readers.

* * * * * * * * * * * * * * * * * * * *

## WANT FREE COPIES OF MY BOOKS?
Just visit my blog and download free copies of my books:
awesomeauthors.org/justplainbob

### About the Publisher

**4Fun Publishing,** a member of **BLVNP Incorporated**, 340 S. Lemon #6200, Walnut CA 91789, info@blvnp.com / legal@blvnp.com
NOTE: Due to the highly emotional reaction of some people to works of erotic fiction, any email sent to the above address that contains foul language or religious references is automatically deleted by our anti-spam software and will not be seen. All other communications are welcome.

### DISCLAIMER

Please don't be stupid and kill yourself. This book is a work of FICTION. Do not try any new sexual practice that you find in this book. It is fiction and not to be confused with reality. Neither the author nor the publisher or its associates assume any responsibility for any loss, injury, death or legal consequences resulting from acting on the contents in this book. Every character in this book is over 18 years of age. The author's opinions are not to be construed as the opinions of the publisher. The material in this book is for entertainment purposes ONLY. Enjoy.

# Gail's Price

## Romance Erotica

By: Just Plain Bob

© **Just Plain Bob 2015**
ISBN: 978-1-68030-478-7

# Chapter 1

I realize now that it was my own fault. I could have been a little more rebellious when I was young and not made promises that I would have to keep. And I could have shown a little more backbone when I met Gail, but that is all water over the dam now.

My mom was always pushing virtue at me and kept trying to impress upon me the importance of entering married life pure, and she made me promise to remain a virgin until my wedding day.

To be honest it wasn't all that hard for me to do. I was pretty shy around girls and I wasn't the most attractive guy around. I was overweight and near-sighted. The bad eyes had me wearing heavy horn-rimmed glasses. I didn't have much of a social life all the way through high school and I didn't even go to the prom.

Things changed in college. My roommate in the dorm took one look at me and decided that I had to change. He was a horn dog and figured that if I was going to be around and we were going to be seen together, he didn't want the girls running the other way when they saw us.

He browbeat me into doing an exercise program and practically forced me at gunpoint into running with him every morning. He convinced me to dump the horn rims and get contacts, and by spring break you could see the results. I'd lost twenty-five pounds (still had fifteen to go) and I felt better about myself.

I was still shy around girls and Mike decided to help me there also although I didn't know about it until way later. What Mike decided was that I was shy around girls because I'd never interacted with them on any level, so he started arranging things to give me more exposure to them. What he did was fix me up without letting me know he was fixing me up.

Typical would be something like, "Hey Rob, I need a huge favor. I have a date with Carol, but she called and told me she had to cancel because her (cousin, sister, best friend—pick one) just came to town. I'm hot for the girl Rob, and I almost had her on our last date. I need to keep the pressure on. Help me out here bud."

"What can I do?"

"Date her (fill in the blank) so my date doesn't get cancelled."

I'd hem and haw, and he would keep on me until I gave in.

Another one was, "Hey Rob, you doing anything Friday night?"

"No."

"I've been invited to a party at Jerry's and I know that Gloria is going to be there. I need a wingman in case she is with one of her sorority sisters. I just know that if I can get her alone I can score. Can you help me out?"

And he would keep after me until I would say yes.

The thing is that it *did* work. The more time I spent in the company of the opposite sex, the more comfortable I became around them; I still lacked the nerve to go after one, but I was no longer shy.

Girls started coming up to me when I was sitting in the school cafeteria and asking if they could join me. They would make small talk about classes and instructors and drop subtle hints that they didn't have dates for this or that party and ask if I was going. Since I wasn't totally brain dead, I would pick up on what they wanted and I would ask them out. I even had a few flat out ask me for a date. As a result I did have a decent social life and I did gain enough confidence in myself that I did finally start asking girls out.

By my junior year I had entered into a relationship with a couple of different girls and I had some pretty hot make out sessions, but as weird as it may sound, both relationships ended when I wouldn't go all the way. I would finger fuck them and Lucinda Welch taught me to eat her pussy, but the most I would allow where my penis was concerned was a hand job. I guess those things weren't exactly pure, but I interpreted my mom as meaning I should remain a virgin—as in not having *actual* intercourse—until I married. Even at twenty my mom's influence still held sway.

"Go to your marriage bed pure Robbie; I'm telling you that you won't regret it."

And her influence stayed current because I was back living at home. Even though Mike wasn't my roommate anymore (you were only required to live in the dorms your freshman year), we still stayed close. We double-dated a lot (still a lot of that "Help me out Rob" going on) and things were going well for me.

I was doing well in class with my GPA hanging around 3.85 and my social life was much better than I ever expected than it would be, given my high school history.

***

It was at a frat/sorority mixer during the third week of my senior year that my life was turned upside down and inside out. I was with Mike, his date and her cousin from out of town when I saw a vision on the other side of the room. It was one of those life defining moments. From the second I laid eyes on Gail Marcella Luoma, no one else in the world existed for me.

I abandoned my date and moved closer to the vision and then followed her, keeping some distance between us, as she moved around the sorority house. Her voice was throaty and sent chills up and down my spine when I heard her speak. Her laugh was musical and she moved with a grace that was enchanting. I was absolutely mesmerized.

It was inevitable that she would notice me—I was that obvious—and when she did, she came over to me.

"Why are you following me around?"

I was caught red-handed and I didn't know what to say, and before I had a chance to think of something she said:

"I don't know who you are and I don't want to know you so knock it off or I'll turn you in to campus security for stalking. Do you understand?"

I nodded a yes and she turned and walked away. I had understood her, but I didn't care. I stopped trying to get close and just watched her from the other side of the room. She noticed, but what could she do? I was a legitimate guest at the party and if we just happened to be in the same room at the same time, there was nothing she could do about it. And as far as campus security? Fuck them! There was no law against looking at beautiful women.

Mike came up to me and asked me what had captured my interest, and I pointed Gail out to him.

"Go up to her and ask her out."

I told him about our small confrontation and he chuckled and said, "Faint heart never won fair lady," and went back to the party.

I made note of the people that Gail talked to, and I knew a few of them so I made a mental note to pump them for information about her.

The party started breaking up and we left. Mike's date's cousin had hooked up with some guy and had left with him earlier so Mike dropped me off at my place and he and his date took off to do whatever it was that they were going to do.

***

"Works for me."

She finished her lunch, opened her purse and took out a note pad and a pen. She wrote on the pad, tore off the page and handed it to me.

"About six okay? Got to run or I'll be late for class."

As Gail walked out of Marvin's, I watched her go and wondered what in the hell had just happened. It made no sense at all to me that she could have gone from the girl at the party to the girl who had just pretty much asked me out. I couldn't figure it out, but I wasn't going to look a gift horse in the mouth either.

*** 

Not wanting anything to keep the date from happening, I made sure that I was in Gail's neighborhood a half an hour early. I wasn't going to let an accident or a traffic jam get in the way. I sat in my car one block over from Gail's place until five to six and then I started up and drove over to her place.

I rang the doorbell right at six and when Gail opened the door, the sight of her took my breath away—she was so beautiful. I offered her my arm and walked her to the car, opened the door and helped her in. Once I was inside the car I asked her what movie she would like to see and was not surprised when she chose a chick flick. I don't even remember the name of it; I was so enthralled just to be sitting next to her. I've mentioned that I had it bad, right?

After the show I asked her if she was hungry and she said she could stand a bite to eat, so I drove over to the malt shop for burgers and fries and then I took her home. I walked her to her door, she kissed me on the cheek and then said:

"Don't be a stranger. Call me, okay?"

She went into the house and I stood there looking at the closed door as I tried to digest the fact that she wanted me to call her. ME! She wanted ME to call her. I don't even remember walking back to the car. SHE wanted ME to call her!

*** 

When I got up the next morning, I took pen in hand and made a list of the things people had told me that she liked and was interested in and then I went looking for them.

She liked art and I found that a gallery in town was having a showing of a new artist, so I called and got dates and times. She liked classical music so I went online and got the schedule for the concert hall. She liked nature and she liked hiking, and my parents had a cabin in the mountains so I called my dad, asked him if I could use it and found out the dates that he wouldn't be there.

Gail was also a bit of a speed freak. She liked NASCAR, dirt track and drag racing and I had a problem with that, in that there wasn't a raceway within two hundred miles of us. I was sure that she had other likes and I was just going to have to dig them out. I checked out my list and noticed that one of the gallery showings was in two days. I went online and found out all that I could about Francis Wheatly (the artist).

I didn't have any shared classes with Gail, but I knew that she usually showed up at the school cafeteria sometime between eleven-forty and eleven fifty-five so I made sure that I was there by eleven-thirty. When I saw Gail come through the line, I waited until she looked my way and I waved at her. I wasn't sure, but I thought I saw a trace of annoyance on her face before she smiled and headed for my table. She sat down and I asked her how she was and she said she was fine.

"I was going to call you tonight, but your being here saves me a phone call. Do you know where the Heritage Gallery is?" I asked.

"I do."

"They are having a show for a new artist named Francis Wheatly. I've heard some good things about him and I was thinking of attending the exhibition. Would you like to go?"

"I would love to. When is it?"

"Tomorrow at seven. Would you like to have dinner before we go?"

"They usually have plenty of munchies at a showing."

"I know, and they are usually pretty fattening, and that is why I like to eat before I go. I can usually pass on the freebies if I've just eaten."

"Good point. Yes; I would like to have dinner before we go."

"Pick you up at five?"

"That'll work for me."

We made the date and then made small talk until we finished lunch, and then we headed off to our classes.

When I got home I called James, a friend of mine who was into art, and found out what showings were like and what some of the dos and don'ts were when you attended one.

*** 

We had dinner at Tricocci's and over dinner she asked what I knew about the artist, and I parroted what I'd read when I Googled his name. She listened and then said:

"I would never have figured you for the type that went to art galleries."

"My parents thought that they should see to it that I was raised with some 'couth,' as they called it, and I was dragged along to a whole bunch of things and some of it actually took. I never could get into ballet or opera, but I did develop a taste for classical music."

"Oh? You have any favorites?"

"Beethoven. I like almost everything he did."

"What is your favorite piece?"

"His concerto for violin and orchestra is by far my favorite, but a close second is his concerto number five. The Emperor."

That was seventy-five percent *bullshit*, as my parents never did anything to expose me to culture, but it was twenty-five percent true because I really did like classical music.

Then we talked about what we were going to do when we graduated. I told her I would be going into the family business and would probably take it over when my father retired. She told me that she was most probably going to go for an MBA and wouldn't even start thinking about a job until she was almost done with her degree program.

The exhibition was interesting, but I didn't much care for Mr. Wheatly's work. He was what was called an impressionist and his stuff had no appeal to me. It did however have some appeal for Gail and there was on piece that she really liked. It had a $500 price tag on it, but James had explained to me how that worked. If you didn't like the price you could have a quiet word with one of the gallery people and put a bid in on the piece. If the piece didn't sell by the end of the show and the artist didn't hold firm on the price, the gallery would call the high bidder and offer the item to him. While Gail was using the bathroom I put in a bid for $325. It really wasn't worth that much as far as I was concerned, but I would try to get it for Gail if I could. I had enough in savings that I could have paid full price, but my dad had taught me not to pay the asking price for anything. "Always bargain" was his motto and he had ingrained it in me.

I paid attention to whatever dad told me because he had never steered me wrong. When I was eight or so and kids were calling me fatso, and four eyes, and I got into pushing and shoving matches with them, dad took me aside and taught me some of the basics of judo and told me to just defend myself, not be the attacker and things would straighten out in a hurry. And he was right. I only had to use what he taught me twice and I was never bothered again.

\*\*\*

When I took Gail home I walked her to the door and she kissed me on the cheek, thanked me for a wonderful weekend and told me to make sure that I called her again.

"I will, but it probably won't be until next week sometime. My folks have a cabin up in the mountains and I told dad I would go up there this weekend and make sure that it was ready for fall. I know for a fact that I'll have to replace some boards on the deck and caulk the windows."

"You are going to the mountains and you aren't going to ask me to go with you?"

"It never occurred to me that you would like to go."

"I love the outdoors. Are there any trails up there to hike?"

"No trails as such, but you can pretty much walk wherever you want."

"Sounds perfect."

"Would you like to go? I'm leaving Friday right after my last class. I need to warn you though. I won't be coming back until Sunday evening and we will be alone for the two nights that we are there."

"And so?"

"Your reputation. You want people knowing that you spent two nights with a guy all alone?"

"Who is going to know? I'm not going to tell anyone. Are you?"

"Of course not."

"I think that you are just afraid to be alone with me."

"There is that."

She kissed me on the cheek again and said, "Call me tomorrow and we can set up the details."

***

The next day after our first class, Mike said he'd heard I'd gone out with Gail.

"Getting anywhere?"

"Two dates so far, and I'm seeing her this weekend."

"Well, all I can say is hang in there bro. I think she might be worth the effort it takes to get her."

I thought that was an odd thing to say, but wrote it off as Mike being Mike.

As the time got closer for my weekend with Gail, I spent hour after hour worrying about it. I'd never spent a weekend alone with a girl before, let alone with a girl that gave me the feelings that Gail did. I was pretty close to being a nervous wreck when I pulled up in front of Gail's place on Friday, but it all went away when I saw Gail's beaming smile when she opened her front door.

On the two hour drive to the cabin we talked about the cabin and the surrounding area and what there was to see and do. I explained to her that we would be truly roughing it. There was no running water or electricity. We carried our water in with us in five gallon jugs and used propane bottles for lighting, cooking and heating. The facilities consisted of an outhouse about a hundred feet from the cabin.

"All it is, is a nice quiet place for a two, three or four day getaway."

"Sounds perfect. Sounds like the kind of place I'd like to get for myself someday."

When we got there, she got out of the pickup, looked around and then said:

"You didn't tell me about the view. It is fantastic."

"That's what it is all about. Dad bought the property and then built the cabin just so he could sit on the deck and enjoy the view."

We carried our stuff inside and she looked around. What she saw was a twelve by twenty foot room with a stair case at the south end that led up into a loft. There were couches against the north and east wall and a table built onto the loft stairway on which a four burner propane stove sat. There was a pot-bellied wood stove in the southeast corner and the floor was the stone of the mountain with a couple of throw rugs on it, but plenty of rock still showed.

After looking around, Gail asked what the sleeping arrangements were.

"You get the bed up in the loft. The sofa on the south wall is a pullout sofa bed and that's where I'll bunk."

She gave me what I thought was a contemplative glance and then carried her bag up to the loft. I fired up the propane stove and fixed us a simple dinner of chicken noodle soup and grilled cheese sandwiches after which we went out and sat on the deck to enjoy the view.

I pointed out a hawk circling off to the east and we watched it for a bit before it suddenly dropped like a rock.

"I guess it is his dinner time too."

I pointed out where my dad had placed a couple of salt blocks near the end of the property and told her that if we were lucky we might see a couple of deer before the weekend was over. The words were no sooner out of my mouth than when two and a fawn did come out of the trees and approached the salt blocks. I looked over at Gail and she was enthralled. I kept my mouth shut and didn't distract her from what she was watching. After a bit the three critters wandered back into the trees and Gail asked:

"Does that happen often up here?"

"Maybe one out of every three times we come up."

By then it was turning dark and the stars started coming out. There is nothing like a star-filled sky when you are in the mountains at 8,900 feet and with no city lights to muddy up the view. I pointed out the Big and Little Dipper and a couple of points of light that I knew were man-made satellites, and while we were looking up an airliner with flashing position lights crossed the sky. He was so far up that the sound of his jet engines never reached us.

"I wouldn't have any problem with living up here full time," Gail said.

"It is rather peaceful," I replied.

We sat there in silence for another half hour and then I got up and went inside the cabin and lit two propane lanterns and then pulled out the bed part of the sofa bed and made it up. Gail came in and I gave her one of the lanterns and told her goodnight. She gave me a funny look and then took the lantern and headed up to the loft.

The next morning, I was up, had the coffee on and was fixing scrambled eggs and bacon when Gail came down the stairs. I poured her a cup of coffee and she sat on the couch and watched me at the stove.

"I can't believe how well I slept last night."

"The clear mountain air does it every time."

"What's on for today?"

"You enjoy yourself while I replace the five bad deck boards and caulk all the windows. Hike around, throw a blanket down and work on your tan, but if you do that use plenty of sunscreen. The sun can get intense in the thinner air up this high."

As we ate our bacon and eggs Gail asked me if I needed any help with what I had to do.

"I didn't bring you up here to work you."

"I would like to hike around, but I don't know the area. I'd rather you walked with me so if I can help you it will let you get done sooner and you can go with me."

"If you put it that way I guess I will let you help."

With Gail's help we finished in around two and then took off on a hike that lasted a little over three hours.

"You hungry yet?" I asked Gail when we were back and sitting on the deck.

"Famished."

There was a stone-lined fire pit just off to the side of the deck and I got a fire going and handed Gail a two foot long sharpened stick.

"What's this for?"

"It is your cooking utensil."

I went into the cabin and came back with a package of hotdogs, a package of hotdog buns and a couple of cold beers. I slid a hotdog onto my sharpened stick and stuck the dog in the fire. Gail followed suit as I said:

"We have marshmallows for desert."

We were sitting there turning our sticks to cook the dogs evenly when suddenly Gail said:

"Look," and pointed up. I looked up and saw a circling hawk. "You think it might be the same one from yesterday?"

"It could be. I read somewhere that hawks are territorial so it could be the one we saw or its mate."

We watched as it circled, but it didn't seem to be finding dinner.

After dinner, cleanup was quick and simple. We broke up the roasting sticks and tossed them into the fire and put the empty beer bottles in the back of the truck. I got two more out of the cooler and we sat on the deck and took in the view. It turned dark and the stars came out and after a bit, Gail asked:

"Do you think there is life up there?"

"Maybe not as we know it, but yes I do believe there is life on other planets. I read somewhere that scientists have identified over eleven hundred planets that have the same relationship with their sun that we have with ours. Roughly the same distance from the sun they revolve around. If you accept the theory of evolution, it would seem impossible that there isn't some kind of life form there."

We sat there in silence for another half hour and then I said it was time for me to turn in. Gail headed for the loft and I settled down on the sofa bed.

The next morning after another breakfast of bacon and eggs we went on another three-hour hike and then we packed up and headed home. Gail was silent and spent a lot of the drive home looking out the passenger side window. When we got to her place she said:

"We just spent two nights in a very romantic setting, but you never tried to hold my hand, put your arm around me or try and kiss me. Why?"

I was silent for a couple of seconds and then said, "Fear."

"Fear? Fear of what?"

"Of doing something that might scare you away. Of doing something that might make you not want me around."

"You can't be serious."

"Of course I am. Don't forget our first meeting and don't forget that you have already said that I come across as a weirdo."

"Jesus! I can't believe that you wasted an entire weekend for something as silly as that."

She slid over next to me, put a hand behind my head and pulled our lips together. She gave me a scorcher of a kiss and when she broke it she said:

"Not bad. Needs some work though. I'm free tomorrow if you want to practice."

"You roller skate?"

"I haven't in years, but yes, I think I can keep my feet under me."

"My last class is at three, so how about I pick you up at five?"

"That works for me as far as tomorrow is concerned, but it is still early. Pull up and go around the corner."

"What?"

"Get us away from the front of the house. I don't want my parents watching me make out."

I pulled around the corner and for the next half hour we did our best to steam up the windows of the truck.

*** 

The next date at Skate City was followed by six more dates, each followed by a steamy make out session. It all ended following a date at the Concert Hall. The date was followed by the usual make out session during which Gail rubbed the lump in my trousers and told me to find a motel room.

I don't think I will ever forget the stunned expression on Gail's face when I said no to her suggestion and then explained why. I don't think it was the "why" that stunned her. It was more likely the "no" that she heard. I doubt that any guy had ever said no to her.

She pulled away from me, tucked her breasts back into her bra and then told me to take her home. I walked her to her door and for the first time since I started dating her I didn't get a kiss or a "Call me."

She might not have said call me, but of course I did call her. Her mother answered the phone and when I asked for Gail her mom said she would check and see if Gail was there. I heard voices in the background and then her mother came back on the phone and told me that Gail wasn't home. She asked me if I would like to leave a message and I told her no. I mean, what would be the point? One of the voices I heard, while mom was "seeing" if Gail was home or not, was Gail's.

The next day I was sitting at a table in the cafeteria when Gail came in. She saw me and then turned around and left. The same thing happened the next day. Friday, when she came in and saw me, she didn't turn and leave. She did keep an eye on me as she went through the line and I wondered if she was going to join me and tell me what was going on, but I should have known better. When she paid the cashier she took her tray and headed for an empty table on the other side of the room.

As I watched her walk toward the table she had chosen I knew that there was no need for her to tell me what was going on because it had happened to me before. Twice! Two other times I'd told a girl no when she had wanted sex and both times I'd been dropped like a hot rock. I watched her sit down, and when two other girls joined her, I got up and headed for my next class.

\*\*\*

Gail may have dropped me, but she still had a hold on me that couldn't be broken. I still had the need to see her and so I started back up with showing up at places where I was likely to see her.

It was three weeks before graduation and I was wondering how I was going to handle my need to see Gail, once I had graduated and was working full time.

I was at a party at Norm Miller's and Gail was there also. She was with a date and he had gotten smashed and had passed out. Some guy I'd never seen before decided to move in on her, but she wasn't having any of it. Every time he would go up to her, she would walk away from him.

Then he fucked up. He walked up to her and started talking and Gail gave him a disgusted look and turned to walk away from him. He reached out, grabbed her arm and pulled her back; Gail tried to get loose from him, but he wouldn't let go. I walked up and said:

"I think the lady wants you to let go of her."

"Butt out dickhead. This ain't none of your business."

"I'm making it my business. Let go of her."

He let Gail go and turned toward me and swung at me. I hadn't had to use the judo my father had taught me since I was eight, but I remembered what to do and the guy ended up on the floor with my knee in the middle of his back and his right arm in a hammer lock.

"Are you going to leave the party quietly or am I going to have to break your arm?"

"Fuck you! My dad's a cop and when…"

"Okay. Broken arm it is," and I began to push his arm up. He yelled in pain and then said:

"Okay, okay I'll leave."

"I'll walk you to the door."

I let him up and I could see that he wanted to take another shot at me and I set myself for it. I guess he noticed and decided that it wouldn't be a good idea and he turned and headed for the front door. I followed along to see that he did leave and I watched until he got in his car and drove away.

Once he was gone I decided that it was time for me to leave and I went looking for Norm, found him and thanked him for the invite. I told him that I'd had a good time and I reminded him that we had a golf date the next morning. He laughed and told me he was going to invite me to every party from now on so he would have someone to put out the trash.

I saw Gail watching us, but I didn't pay any attention to her and left the party shortly thereafter.

***

I didn't realize it at the time, but others had taken note of my infatuation with Gail and had also witnessed what I'd done at the party; and the word had gone out that you should not mess with Gail if I was around. Not that you couldn't date her, but best that you didn't get pushy or grab her if she clearly didn't want it.

Over the next several days I'd be in the cafeteria when Gail would occasionally come in; and while she never approached me, she sat where she could see me and she watched me—or at least it seemed to me that she did.

It was two weeks after Norm's party and I was at a kegger at the Kappa Tau house. We were having a pre-graduation party a week before the big day, and an hour into the party, Gail came in with Joel Mack. Joel was on the basketball team and he was good. Probably pro quality, and he had an inflated ego. He thought he was King Shit, if you know what I mean.

Joel proceeded to get drunk on his ass, and the drunker he got the more he treated Gail like she was his to do with as he pleased. As his behavior got worse it was obvious that Gail was getting more and more pissed at him, and it finally reached the point where he said something to her and she slapped his face. He yelled, "You fucking bitch" and he went to hit her.

I'd been doing my watching thing as usual, and as things had gotten louder between Gail and Joel I had moved closer and I was close enough that when he raised his hand to hit her, I was close enough to jump forward and grab his arm. Keep in mind here that all I was thinking of was protecting Gail and wasn't thinking of anything else. Things like: I was only five eleven and Joel was six eight, and two twenty to my one eighty-five and, even drunk, he had good reflexes. The result was me on the floor on my ass with a bloody nose. Fortunately for me there were cooler heads present and they acted. A drunken brawl could put the house on probation and cause the star of the basketball team to be suspended, so several guys grabbed Joel and hustled him out of the house.

I didn't look at Gail as I got up and headed for the bathroom to clean up and put a cold rag on my nose. I got the bleeding stopped, and when I came out of the bathroom I quickly left the house. I didn't want to face the sneers and jeers I expected to be sent my way.

***

The party had been on a Friday so it was Monday before I was back to school. I expected some finger-pointing and laughter, and was surprised when I didn't get any.

I was in the cafeteria at lunch, sitting by myself as usual, when Mike joined me.

"Hear you got into it with that idiot basketball player."

"Don't know how much into it I got. All I know is that my ass hit the floor."

"Whatever dude, but I hear that all the ladies there are thinking pretty highly of you right now."

"I doubt that. I must have looked like a clown sitting on the floor with blood running down my face."

"It wasn't what you looked like that got to them dude. It is what you did that got you put on the floor. You took on a dude twice your size to stop him from hitting a girl."

"Yeah bro, they will all flock to me now. I can just see it. In my dreams."

I changed the subject and a couple of minutes later I saw Gail come into the cafeteria. She saw me sitting with Mike and I expected her to find a table on the other side of the room, but when she left the cashier she headed right for my table. Mike saw her coming and said:

"I'll get out of here so she can sit with her knight in shining armor."

"Yeah! Right!"

He got up and left and Gail came up and asked me if she could join me. Was I going to say no?

She sat down, looked at me in silence for several seconds and then said:

"How are you going to protect me after we graduate and the two of us don't go to the same places anymore?"

I didn't know what to say so I just looked at her. She waited, and when I didn't say anything, she said:

"We need to talk Rob, and I don't mean a short conversation here at the table. Can you pick me up tonight around six? We can go some place for a bite and have a serious talk."

I sat there trying to think of what she was planning to do to me when she said:

"Come on Rob, say something."

I finally got myself together and said, "I don't know that we have anything to talk about. The way you dropped me pretty much told me where I stand with you. I don't know if I can put up with another put down."

"That's what we need to talk about. Come on Rob. A couple of hours with me won't kill you."

*That's what you think,* I told myself. The truth was a couple of hours with her that ended like our last date did could very well kill me. Or kill my spirit anyway. But I was so hooked on her that regardless of what she might do I had to say yes just to spend some time in her presence. I told her I would pick her up at six and then I got up and headed for class.

***

To say I was curious as to what Gail wanted to talk about would be an understatement. The way she had dumped me without a word was sitting heavily on me, but then I had to remember the girl had a way with sudden surprises. I thought back to our initial meeting followed by her basically asking me out.

I had no idea of what to expect when I walked up on her porch and rang her doorbell. She opened the door, gave me a dazzling smile and said:

"Right on time as usual. I guess there is something to be said for someone so reliable. Where are we going?"

"This is your idea so I thought I'd let you choose."

"Then I choose Tricocci's. I like their Veal Marcella."

On the way to the restaurant we talked about what we would be doing when we ended the school portion of our lives and the conversation carried on over dinner. Once the meal was out of the way, over coffee Gail said:

"I really do like you Rob, and my feelings were well on the way to being stronger—much stronger—than just like, and then you hit me with the promise that you made your mother."

I started to say something, but she cut me off.

"Just let me talk Rob. You can speak your piece when I get done, but I want to get it all out without interruptions. You telling me that you wouldn't engage in love-making until you got married caused me to pull back from you. I haven't been a virgin since I turned eighteen Rob, and I like sex. Hell, I adore sex and I can barely go a week without having some. That's the problem Rob—I need sex and you just won't do it. If you were to ask me to marry you tonight and I were to say yes, it would take my mom six months to plan the wedding and there is no way in hell that I could go six months without sex.

"Finger-fucking and hand jobs are not sex as far as I'm concerned; they are merely foreplay. To be blunt Rob, I need to be fucked and I need it on a regular basis, and because of your promise to your mother I can't get it from you."

"That is why you wanted me to take you out tonight? So you could tell me this?"

"Yes. I guess you could say I'm trying to set you free."

"Trying to set me free?"

"It is obvious from what happened at Norm's party and what happened at the frat house that you are always going to try and be around me, so I am telling you that you are wasting your time. You have no chance with me. Well, maybe one. If we could get married in the next three or four days, but that can never happen because my mom would kill me if I didn't let her go all-out in planning the wedding.

"So what this date is about is my trying to keep you from wasting your time. Don't get me wrong. I think it is sweet that you care for me as much as you do, and if it wasn't for your promise to your mother I think we would be good together. Actually I think we would be great together."

"You say you can barely go a week without making love, but you dated me for a couple of weeks and we didn't have sex."

"You didn't, but I did."

What that meant hit me right in the pit of my stomach.

"You mean…"

"I didn't go out with you every night Rob and I rarely stayed home on those nights."

She saw the look on my face and said, "Don't be that way Rob. We were just dating. We were not going steady or anything like that. We had no commitment to each other."

"No hope for me at all?"

"I'm sorry Rob, I really am. I wish I could say that there was, but there isn't. I know myself too well to even try and go from now until we could get married without having sex."

I called for the tab, paid it and then drove Gail home in silence. I walked her to her door, and when she went up on her toes to kiss me, I turned my head so the kiss landed on my cheek and then I turned and left. When I got home, there was a message for me on the answering machine. The gallery had called to let me know that my bid on the painting Gail had liked had been accepted.

*Great timing,* I thought. *Just fucking great.*

Saturday I went to the gallery, paid for the painting and then paid extra to have the painting packaged and shipped to Gail. I hoped that she would think of me every time she looked at it and wonder about what could have been.

Thursday I walked across the stage, received my sheepskin and headed into the next portion of my life. My parent's graduation present to me was a one year lease on a two bedroom condo and the furniture to fill it. I spent the weekend moving in and on Monday I started my full time job in the family business.

I'd worked there summers since I was fourteen so there wasn't any "new guy" break in period. I already knew the people that I would be working with so I was able to hit the ground running. And speaking of running, I'd never stopped since Mike got me started. I ran nearly every morning and I was in the best physical shape of my life. I knew that sitting behind a desk all day wasn't going to help me stay in that shape and that just running wasn't going to be enough.

There was a gym two blocks from the office and I joined and started working out on my lunch hours on Monday, Wednesday and Friday. Turns out that one hour just wasn't enough time for a workout when you subtracted the time it took to get there, the time it took to shower after the work out and the time it took to get back to the office; so I started going in at five in the morning when they opened. It worked out so well for me that I started going in every morning.

The gym also had classes during the day and in the evenings for everything from spinning to tai chi chuan, and I decided to take the class on tai chi two nights a week when I got off work.

*** 

The Fates or whatever Gods must be getting some sort of perverse pleasure out of fucking over mere mortals like me.

It was the third week since I started the tai chi class and I got to the gym at my normal time, and on the way to the men's locker room I had to pass by the circuit machine and free weights area. I happened to glance in—and saw Gail working out on the seated leg press. She saw me, and I looked away from her and hurried to the locker room.

That night's tai chi class was wasted on me. Tai chi is all about concentrating on your inner core and I could not concentrate for shit. As hard as it was to do I'd thought I had made some progress on putting Gail behind me—and now here she was, back in the forefront of my mind. Luckily she was gone when I got out of class and I didn't have to try and avoid her.

On my way home, I wondered if I was going to have to drop the class to keep from having to see her; which was a one hundred and eighty-degree change from when I was in school and did everything in my power to be where I could see her. The difference of course was that back then I had hope. However thin it was, it was still hope, but she had crushed that hope on our last date.

The Fates and the Gods were not done with me yet.

The next day at work I was in my office reviewing contracts when Marva, the secretary I shared with three others, called me on the intercom and told me that there was someone from Ferris Industries there to see me. I was expecting a contract from Ferris and I had thought it was going to be sent over by messenger, but I guess that John over at Ferris thought that it was important enough to be hand delivered. I told Marva to send the visitor in.

The door opened and I moaned, "Fuck me."

"I'd love to," Gail said as she walked into my office. "May I sit down?"

"Please do," I said.

"First off," Gail said, "I had no idea I would be delivering this contract to you," she said as she handed me the envelope. "I didn't even know that you worked here. But I'm glad because now I can thank you for the painting you sent me.  I didn't even realize that you knew I liked it.  I do have a question for you though.  How did you find out I worked at the gym?"

"I didn't know.  I work out there every morning and I only started taking the evening tai chi class a few weeks ago."

"Why am I having a hard time believing that?"

"Maybe because you don't want to believe it."

"Why would I not want to believe it?"

"Maybe you got used to me being close by and it bothers you that I haven't been since graduation.  Maybe you don't want to believe it because you are wishing that I would be around.  I don't know if either of those is true or not, but you can check with Nancy, the morning girl behind the entry desk, and she can tell you when I joined and when I come in to work out."

"You might be right.  Maybe I'm having a hard time believing that someone so desperate to just see me, that he hung around every place he thought I would be, could just quit and disappear."

"Quit and disappear?  Have you forgotten our last date?  You did the verbal equivalent of kicking me in the balls.  Of course I got the message.  The night you dropped me like a hot rock added to what you laid on me on our last date came through loud and clear.  Believe me lady; if I had known that you worked out at that gym, I never would have joined."

"That from a guy so desperate to see me that he became my shadow?"

"No.  That from a guy who could not bear to look at you knowing that there was absolutely no hope for him.  It was one thing when there was a smidgen of hope.  It was something else again to know that there was absolutely none."

"You would have rather I'd said nothing so you could go on wasting your time?"

I just shrugged and said, "Thank you for bringing the contract. Tell Mr. Stiles I'll review it and get back to him sometime tomorrow afternoon."

Gail sat there and looked at me for several seconds and then she got up and left.

*Why me God*, I said to myself as the door closed behind her.  *Why don't you go and fuck with someone else.*

***

My friendship with Mike had continued after graduation and I had dinner with him that evening after work.

"You seem down," he said as I picked away at my meal.

"I had a bummer of a day."

"Hey dude, it is only work.  You get to walk away from it at five o'clock."

"It wasn't work.  Gail stopped in at the office today.  I was making progress at getting over her and then there she was sitting across from me in my office."

"I'm sorry Rob."

"What do you have to be sorry for?"

"For getting you mixed up with her."

couldn't see it, but I would have been willing to bet big money that she knew it was there.

"We seemed destined to run into each other," she said.

I could have just shrugged and kept my mouth shut, but I decided that sticking my head in the sand and pretending that she wasn't there would be a waste of time since she knew that I was hung up on her, so I said:

"I'm not going to complain, but couldn't you have at least toned down the impact by wearing a tank suit instead of that bikini?"

"Tone it down?  Why would I do that?  This suit was designed to get attention and that is why I wear it."

"I thought that you didn't want my attention.  At least that was the impression I got when you stopped dating me."

She was silent for a few seconds and then in a soft voice said:

"Things change."

"In what way?"

"I told you on our last date that my feelings for you were getting stronger than just like, and I guess that they were stronger than I realized. I've not gone a day since that last date that I haven't thought of you.  It was a happy surprise to find out that we belong to the same gym, but it wasn't by accident that I delivered that contract to you.  I knew you worked there, and when my boss told me to call the messenger service to send over the contract, I told him I knew you and that I would like to bring it over so I could say hi."

"Why?"

"To put myself in a place where communication could happen."

I said nothing and just swiped my membership card through the card reader and headed for the men's locker room. I had no idea what Gail's program was, but I hoped that she worked the circuit machines first. That way I could avoid her because I usually started with cardio on the treadmill which was at the other end of the building from the circuit and free weight area.

Naturally, I didn't get what I wanted. There were five treadmills in the cardio section and Gail was on the one in the center which meant that no matter which of the other four I chose Gail was going to be almost right next to me. I could have just turned and gone to the circuit area, but why? I needed to face up to the fact that if Gail was going to be around, the only way to avoid her would be to quit working out at the gym and find another one.

But who did I think I was kidding. Certainly not myself. Yes, I had started trying to put Gail behind me after graduation, but she was still there in my mind and I thought of her often. I was able to survive her dropping me and still go where I could manage to see her and now here she was only eight feet away. I knew that nothing would come of it, but she was where I could be around her now so I was going to take the gift that the Fates and the Gods had given me.

I did my usual fifteen minutes on the treadmill and then moved to the circuit area to begin the rest of my workout. I was not at all surprised when a couple of minutes later Gail showed up. We hadn't said a word to each other when we were on the treadmills and we didn't talk as we worked our way through the fourteen machines. Didn't talk, but I watched her and she knew I didn't take my eyes off of her.

When I finished my routine I headed for the locker room and changed into my swimming trunks and went to the steam room where I spent just over eight minutes before heading for the hot tub. I'd no sooner sat down in the 105 degree water when Gail showed up and joined me in the tub. She was wearing a bikini; and seeing her in it gave me instant wood. Fortunately with all the bubbles and the swirling water Gail

"No bud. I'm an asshole, but not *that* big of an asshole. I screw the babes, not my buds. She did come back though, but only to cuss me out."

"For what?"

"Messing with her mind. She said I'd set her up with a good guy even though I knew it wouldn't go anywhere. She was really pissed when she told me that, and I didn't have a clue as to what she was talking about."

"I guess that explains it. I wondered at her sudden turn around. Now I know."

Suddenly it dawned on me that Gail wasn't the first one Mike had sent my way. I remembered back to when girls started coming up to me in the cafeteria and asking if they could join me. I didn't know if I should scream at Mike for helping fuck my life up, or thank him for making it possible for getting what little I did get.

\*\*\*

The next trick the Fates and the Gods played on me was the next morning. I showed up at the gym at ten to five and I was standing there waiting for Nancy to open the door when a voice behind me said:

"Good morning."

I turned and saw Gail standing there.

"I decided that early mornings would work better for me."

"I don't believe it. I think you just want to torment me."

Before she could reply, Nancy opened the doors and we followed her to the front desk. "Decided to bring your wife with you," Nancy asked.

Gail laughed and said, "He wishes."

"What do you mean by that?"

"Nothing bud."

"Oh no you don't Mike. You can't say that and expect me to just let it pass. What did you mean when you said you were sorry for getting me mixed up with her?"

He was silent and I said, "Come on Mike, spit it out."

He shrugged and then said, "You know I'm a horndog and a bit of an asshole where girls are concerned right?"

I nodded a yes.

"The reason I went through so many girls had nothing to do with my manly charm. To put it bluntly I'm rather well hung. I didn't have to chase the girls. Mostly they chased me. I guess girls talk among themselves the same as guys do. Anyway, the word spread about my package and girls would come up to me and ask if it was true and my response was always "There is only one way you will find out" and four out of every five said "Let's get to it.""

"Gail was one of the girls who came to me and asked the question. I knew you were hung up on her and you had already told me about the first time she had talked to you, so instead of giving her my standard response I told her the only way she would ever find out was if she did me a favor and cut you a break."

"Cut me a break?"

"Yeah. Talk to you. Be civil and like that."

"So after she made nice with me she came back to you and sampled the goods?"

"Again, why?"

"Do I have to carve it into your chest?! I've missed you dummy! That's why!"

"I've missed you too, but nothing has changed. I still intend to keep my promise to my mother."

"I admit that is a problem, but maybe we can work around it."

"How do we do that?"

"We will think of something. So! Do you ask me or do I have to ask you?"

"Ask what?"

"For a date, you blockhead!"

"A date? You and me?"

"No. Me and your mother. Of course you and me."

I have to admit that I was surprised and I just sat there and looked at her as I tried to process what had just happened. I don't know how she took my silence, but apparently she thought I wasn't going to ask her so she said:

"Okay. I'll do it. Would you like to have dinner with me tonight?"

I might have been sitting there confused, but I'm not a complete dummy so I answered:

"Of course I would."

"Pick me up at six?"

"I'll be there."

*** 

I rang her doorbell right at six and when she opened the door she took my breath away the same as she did the first time I'd picked her up. I remembered how much she had enjoyed the Veal Marcella at Tricocci's so that is where I took her.

Over dinner we talked about adjusting to life after sixteen years of school. She had decided against going for an MBA and she liked her job and was looking for a place of her own. I was almost tempted to tell her she could move into my spare bedroom, but I didn't because I was afraid she would think I was pushing too hard; it might push her away and that is the last thing I wanted to happen.

We had both turned twenty-one since our last date and so I took her to The Pit for drinks and dancing. God but did I ever like the feel of her in my arms, and her body pressing against mine had predictable results and she felt it, smiled and said:

"I don't think your mother would approve of that."

I wisely did not respond to that.

We left the lounge around ten-thirty and she had me pull over and park a block from her house. She slid over next to me and said "Kiss me" and I did. I did for the next twenty minutes. When I walked her to her door she kissed me again and said:

"I have something I need to do tomorrow, but I'm free the rest of the week."

"Day after tomorrow?"

"You have a date," and she kissed me again.

***

By the end of our fourth date we were back to finger fucking and hand jobs. It was on our tenth date and I was parked the usual block from her house when she asked me:

"How do you interpret virginity?"

"I beg your pardon?"

"Easy enough question, sugar. How do you define virginity?"

The question stumped me because I'd never given any thought to it.

"Let me help you out a little bit. You don't seem to mind playing with my pussy and you haven't shoved my hands away when I give you hand jobs. Do you see putting your dick into my pussy as the only way to lose your cherry?"

"I've never thought on it."

"Then let me ask you this. Would my giving you a blow job be any different than my giving you a hand job?"

I thought for a minute and then said, "I don't honestly know. I guess I've always assumed that making love for the first time is when you give up your virginity."

"That's the way I see it too. I've already told you about my high sex drive and that I can't go without sex for as long as it would take my mother to plan the wedding. I think I can get by if you eat my pussy. If you will do that I will of course suck your dick. It is the orgasms that I get from having sex that drive me. If you can give me those orgasms by eating me I should be okay. What do you think?"

"I don't know. I've only done it a couple of times so I don't really know how good I'd be at it."

"I can teach you how, sugar. It isn't a hard thing to do. Want to give it a try?"

I thought about it for a bit and then said, "I'm willing to try."

"Tonight?"

My answer was to start the truck and drive past her house as I headed for my condo. I had never mentioned my condo to Gail so she was surprised when we got there.

"I thought you still lived at home and that we were on our way to a motel."

"Mom and dad kicked me out. This is their bribe to get me to leave without a fuss."

Once inside, she looked around and then said, "That painting that you gave me would look just right on that wall," and she pointed at the east wall of the living room. I'd been meaning to get some art work for the walls and so I said:

"Maybe, but it is your picture so if I was to put it on that wall you would have to come with it."

"It could happen sugar, but a few things have to happen first."

"Like what?"

"Let's count them off. First, a proposal and a ring. Next, we tell my mom so she can get started on the wedding she has been expecting to give me since I was sixteen. There is one other thing that comes between the proposal and us telling my mom, but I will leave it for later."

"Why?"

"Because I need to lock you in and make sure that we are firmly attached before bringing it up. Now, would you care to sit down on the couch with me and neck until we get hot enough to do what we came here for?"

I found out that I enjoy the hell out of blowjobs and I also found out that Gail thinks I have talent when it comes to eating pussy. Following her instructions, I was able to get her off. Twice!

Following that night we saw each other three or four times a week and after a month and a half of joint oral sex I bowed to the inevitable and bought a ring.

We were at my condo following an evening of dinner, drinks and dancing, and I took a knee and asked the question.

I did not get the response I expected.

"I would love to sugar. I would love to and I really do want to, but I have a condition and I don't know if you will be willing to meet it."

"We won't know until you tell me what it is."

"Remember way back when I told you that I couldn't go a week without sex? Well that hasn't changed any. I thought that the orgasms from oral would hold me, but they haven't."

"But…"

"Let me finish sugar. I need to get this out into the open. I want you. I really do want to be your wife, but you are holding steadfast to the promise you made your mom. That, by the way, is one of the things I love about you. The fact that you have integrity. But it is also a curse because it keeps you from giving me the sex I need. I'm not lying when I say that it will probably take my mom six months to plan and put the wedding together and I cannot go six months without sex. You are fantastic when it comes to eating my pussy, but it isn't enough to hold me.

"There are some things I will not do and cheating is one of them. My seeing other guys and having sex with them is not cheating, at least not yet, because you and I are not in a committed relationship, so my seeing others is not cheating on you. At least it isn't, as far as I'm concerned. If I say yes and accept your ring and still saw other guys for the sex I need, it would be cheating. It would be cheating unless you were okay with it. If I say yes, you would have to be okay with me seeing someone else once or twice a week until we could consummate our marriage, and I honestly do not think that you can do that."

"You mean you have been making love with other guys all the time we have been dating?"

"No sugar, not making love; just fucking; and believe it or not there *is* a difference."

I knelt there, ring in hand, and tried not to show how pissed off and angry I was. I stood, put the ring in my pocket and offered my hand to Gail. She gave me a questioning look, took my hand and I pulled her up off the couch and walked her to the door.

"What are you doing?"

"Taking you home."

"It doesn't need to be this way Rob."

"Of course it does Gail."

I got her in the truck and drove her home in silence. I walked her to her door, and when she went to kiss me I turned and walked away without a word.

When I got home I went to bed, but I didn't sleep for shit. I cursed the Fates and the Gods for what they were doing to me. I skipped the gym in the morning because I figured that Gail would be there, and the last thing I needed at the time was to see her. It would only remind me that the woman who owned me, body and soul, would never be mine.

# Chapter 2

I lost myself in work and fortunately there was so much of it that I never had a free moment to spend thinking about Gail.

I hadn't been home five minutes when the phone rang and caller ID showed that it was Gail. I didn't take the call, or any of the four others that came after it, before unplugging the phone and going to bed.

I skipped gym the next morning for the same reason I had skipped the day before, and instead went for my run in the morning rather than in the evening after work as was my usual habit. During the run I realized that unless I changed gyms there was no way I could avoid Gail. Plus I was doing well with my tai chi and I didn't want to give it up and have to start all over with another instructor. So, hoping that Gail was still going to the gym in the mornings, I sucked it up and showed up for my tai chi class that evening—and for a change, the Fates and the Gods didn't screw with me.

Until class was over and I got back to my truck.

Sitting on my right front fender was Gail. I stopped about ten feet from the truck and just stood there and looked at her.

"We need to talk Rob."

"I thought that everything that needed to be said was covered the other night."

"No it wasn't. You need to hear me out. It won't hurt any to give me my say."

"Horse shit Gail. You have already hurt me with what you have already said.

"Then the damage is done, so what I still have to say won't hurt you any worse."

I figured that she would keep after me until I gave in, so I thought I might as well get it over with.

"Okay Gail. Go ahead and speak your piece."

"Can we get in the truck? I don't want people passing by to hear what I'm saying."

I hit the button on the remote to unlock the doors and we got in the truck.

"First off," she started, "Give me credit for being totally up front and honest with you Rob. I know you won't look at it the way I do, but ask yourself if anything I did when I was away from you hurt us. No it did not. Granted, you didn't know about it, but you had no need to know because as I told you once before we were not in a committed relationship. You offered me a committed relationship and I was totally honest with you.

"I want that relationship Rob. I really do want your ring on my finger; but like I told you, I will not cheat on you, but I have my needs. Can't you understand that?"

"Of course I can understand it, but what you asked of me was that I condone what you would be doing to meet those needs. You were asking me to let my fiancée fuck other guys. Just what kind of guy would that make me? A cuckolded wimp is what. No way, Gail. No fucking way!"

"You are not a wimp Rob and I'm fully aware of it. A wimp wouldn't have tried to protect me the way you have, and 'cuckold' is just a made up word and it means nothing. It is just a word that will be inside your head, and no one is going to call you a cuckold because no one is going to know. I don't do anything with anyone you know and I don't do it around people who know the both of us.

"You want me Rob, and I want you. All I'm asking is that you let me do what I need to do to let us happen. It doesn't even need to be twice a week Rob. May be once every two or three weeks. I don't really know. I've never tried to go for any length of time without it. I don't know because I have no frame of reference since I've never had to go without. I wouldn't rub your face in it. I wouldn't tell you when I was going to do it. It would only be at times when we weren't together and it wouldn't necessarily be all the times we weren't together so you wouldn't know when.

"The main thing is that I would not be cheating because you would be aware. I want you Rob, but I will not, absolutely will not, cheat on you. We cannot happen if you cannot accept what I need to do. Just remember this Rob: I could have said yes and taken your ring, and then told you that I play cards with some of my sorority sisters every Tuesday or Wednesday night, and used those nights to scratch my itch with you being none the wiser—but I won't do that to my man. Once again Rob; I will not cheat!

"I want you Rob and I believe that you want me. You are the only one who can decide on how bad you want me. I'm yours if you can do what it takes," and she got out of the truck and walked away.

\*\*\*

Lying on my bed staring up at the ceiling, I went over what Gail had said. I *did* want her—but bad enough to do what she said I'd have to do? I thought about the periods when I'd dated her and she had seen to "her needs" both times, and she was right in that it had never hurt us, but that was only because I hadn't known. Would it have hurt us if I had known? I didn't have an answer for that.

Like most red-blooded guys in this age of computers, I'd cruised the Net and visited porn sites and I'd visited story sites and read some of the stories. In the cheating stories the guys always ended up asking themselves why the woman did it. Weren't they getting the job done? Wasn't their dick big enough and stuff like that, but I wasn't in the same situation. My prowess or lack thereof didn't enter in to it because we had never made love.

Yes, I was pissed and angry when I heard what she had done, but I couldn't overlook the fact that it was Gail herself who had told me and I did have to accept that she was being up front and honest with me about it all.

I woke up in the morning at three AM and couldn't go back to sleep so I put on my running shoes and went for an early morning run. My runs served a dual purpose. They helped keep me fit and it helped clear the cobwebs out of my head. I could usually think a little more clearly after a run.

When I got home I grabbed my gym bag and the garment bag with the clothes I would wear to work and headed for the gym. I wasn't going to spend my life ducking Gail, so facing up to the situation needed to start now.

Gail was already standing in front of the doors waiting for them to open when I got there, so I sat in the truck until Nancy opened up to let the people in and didn't get out of the truck until Gail went inside. I wasn't going to avoid being where she was, but I saw no need in putting myself in a situation where we could stand around together and give her another chance to talk to me.

Gail wasn't in the circuit room so I assumed that she was down in cardio and I decided to do the machines first. I was on the last machine, the one called "Rear Row Deltoids" and just finishing the last of my hundred reps when Gail came into the area. She called out "Good morning Rob" and I acknowledged her with a nod, got up and headed for cardio.

I'd had a good run that morning so I took a pass on the treadmill and opted for the Stairmaster. After fifteen minutes of that I headed for the locker room, put on my trunks and headed for the hot tub only to find that Gail was already there. It was a big hot tub and could seat up to twenty-four so I didn't need to sit within talking distance of Gail. I sat down as far from her as I could get, leaned back, closed my eyes and soaked.

The swirling water, bubbles and the noise of the jets masked the approach of Gail and I had no idea she was sitting close to me until she said:

"I didn't sleep well last night, Rob. All I could do was lie there and think about what might have been, or maybe I should say *could have been*, or even more accurately, what *should have been*."

I opened my eyes and looked at her for a couple of seconds before saying:

"And whose fault is that, Gail? You are the one who can't keep your legs closed; and don't give me any of that horse shit about how you can't go a week without sex. You could if you wanted to, but the fact of the matter is that you don't want to. You try and sell the song and dance that it wouldn't be cheating if I were to go along with it and that is absolute bullshit. If you are in a relationship with someone and are fucking someone else, you *are* cheating! Period!

"There might be some warped dudes out there who can accept it when their woman fucks someone else, but I'm not one of them. My woman has to be mine and mine alone. I will not share! You can't commit to me and that's on you Gail. If you can't sleep because of your actions, that is *your* tough luck and not mine."

I got out of the hot tub, showered, dressed and went to work.

***

For the next two weeks I saw Gail everyday Monday through Friday, and while she never did try to talk to me, I do have to admit that I couldn't take my eyes off of her. What had started that day in college still held; I had to see her. There was something deep inside me that required that visual fix.

I spent a lot of time thinking about how unfair life was. To want something so bad and to know it could be yours if only you were a little more accommodating. It was unbelievable how many rationalizations I was able to come up with that would let me give in to what Gail said she required. Everything from a simple "Why should I care. I'm not using it" to a more complicated "If you really want something bad enough, shouldn't you be willing to pay the cost?"

I knew Gail was my other half the instant I laid eyes on her for the first time and every minute that I'd spent in her company since then had only solidified that belief. So why couldn't I do what she wanted? What could it hurt? It would get me what I wanted. What I craved. It really hadn't hurt us when we dated right? And I wouldn't even know when she was doing it. Just that it might—only might—happen on the nights we didn't spend together. And she had said that it would never be with anyone I knew or around anyone who knew the both of us. Those were the thoughts roaring through my head as I tried to make myself do what I needed to do to make Gail mine.

And then one morning I woke up and faced a few things. If she couldn't go a week without, what would she do if we were married and I wasn't around? And that would happen. I knew going into it that my job was going to eventually require travelling on business. There were industry conventions, seminars and the like that would be out of town and require me to be gone a week or two. What if I got hurt and was unable to perform for a couple of weeks? And what if my sex drive wasn't as strong as hers? I had some dark thoughts. Dark thoughts indeed.

\*\*\*

I guess I really wasn't as strong and firm as my "I won't share!" statement indicated. I kept sliding closer and closer to the precipice. It came to a head on a Friday three weeks after I'd gotten out of the hot tub and stormed off leaving Gail behind.

I was again in the hot tub following my work-out and about five minutes after I'd sat down Gail joined me. She sat down away from me, but still close enough to talk, and after a minute or two of silence she said:

"I've missed you Rob. Can't we at least be friends?"

I wanted to be more—much, much more—than just friends, but I didn't say that. What I said was:

"We will always be that, Gail."

"Maybe close enough friends that we could occasionally date?"

The plaintive tone of her voice struck a chord in me, and my downfall started with an:

"I don't see why not."

When I left the tub to dress and go to work, I had a date for that evening.

In the following three weeks, I went out with Gail nine times, and at the end of the third week we went up to my parent's cabin for the weekend—and the last nail was driven into my coffin: I let Gail talk me into sleeping with her. Just sleeping. No love-making. When we got there, I told her the sleeping arrangements would be the same as before, with her taking the bed in the loft and me using the sofa bed, but at bedtime she said:

"Sleep with me Rob. Please? I'll be good. I won't push anything. I just want to be held. To snuggle up to you and cuddle."

I said yes, and when I woke up the next morning with Gail wrapped around me, I knew that I would do whatever I had to do to keep us together.

I didn't jump right out and say, "Okay Gail; I'll accept your conditions." Another two weeks went by and I listened to her trying to talk me into what she wanted and I did spend a lot of time thinking on it. Then on a Friday night date she said:

"Please Rob. I'll do my best not to do anything. I can't promise, but I'll do my absolute best. I swear I will."

As I've said, I'd given it a lot of thought and it all boiled down to "Was I willing to pay the price for what I wanted?" and in the end the answer was yes. But was *she*? And the answer to that one was no. She was not willing to give up fulfilling her desires in order to get me. But would she be willing to suffer some humiliation? It was time to find out.

In all the thinking I had been doing, there had been some dark thoughts as well, and those dark thoughts were going to be dropped onto the table. When she finished saying "I'll do my best Rob; I swear I will," I said:

"I guess I can give it a try Gail, but I do have some conditions that will have to be met."

"Conditions? What are they?"

"The first one is a matter of trust. I am only willing to go along with you because of your upfront honesty about what you have been doing, and will probably continue doing your absolute best notwithstanding. I am counting on that honesty to continue. So the first condition is that you never lie to me. No lies Gail; not even little white ones and no evasions if I ask questions.

"Next you will never break a date with me to be with one of your fuck buddies."

She started to say something, but I cut her off with, "You can have your say when I finish. If you break a date with me, you should know that I will suspect that it is so you can see someone else to take care of those needs you keep throwing up to me; so you need to be very careful, Gail. Very, very careful; because a date broken with me could very well kill us off. If we set up a date for, say a Tuesday, and you break, it most likely will be the kiss of death. However, if I ask for a date on Tuesday and you say you can't, that will be acceptable.

"Next on my list is that from Friday after work until midnight Sunday you are mine. These are my days exclusively and family functions are the only acceptable excuse for not giving me those days.

"This last one is the biggie. As long as you are seeing other guys I will no longer perform oral sex on you, since I could very easily pick up with my mouth whatever diseases some other guy might give you. You have heard it said that when you have sex with someone, you are having sex with everyone that person has had sex with, right? Three days before the wedding you will have to give me a report from a reputable local doctor or lab stating that you are disease free."

"How can you ask me to do that? I thought you loved me. Asking me to do that is just disgusting."

"Now you know how I feel about what you are asking me to do. Anyway, those are my conditions. If you want us to go forward you will accept them. You accept them and I'll slide a ring on your finger and you can turn your mother loose to do her thing."

"I'm going to need to think about this."

"No you don't, Gail. If you want us together as bad as you say you do, there is nothing to think about. If you really do need to think about it, I'll take it to mean that your feelings for me are not as strong as they need to be for us to be in a committed relationship. If you can't say "Of course I accept Rob; anything to get you" then both of us are wasting each other's time and we need to put an end to things and get on with our lives.

"This is our defining moment, Gail. What you say in the next thirty seconds will determine the start of our futures. We will move into those futures either together or singly. Your call."

Gail sat looking at me for maybe ten seconds and then she finally said:

"You know I have to accept Rob. I know we belong together and I will do what I have to do to make it happen."

"All right then. Gail Marcella Luoma, will you marry me?"

"Yes, Rob, I will."

I reached into my pocket for the ring and then I reached for her left hand and said:

"I already did the knee thing," as I slid the ring on her finger, "And while this might not seem like an overly romantic moment, it is a totally sincere gesture on my part."

"It is good enough for me Rob. The important thing, at least to me, is that I now have your ring on my finger."

The next day Gail took me to meet her parents. I hadn't met them before, but I had talked to her mother several times on the phone when calling Gail. They seemed very nice and I didn't sense any displeasure as to their daughter's choice for a mate.

Gail's dad asked if we had picked a date for the wedding yet, and Gail said:

"It is up to mom. She has been talking about what she was going to do wedding wise for the last four years. If it were up to me, I'd get the license and blood tests done, and have a civil ceremony next week."

"Oh no you won't," her mother said and got up and left the room. She came back a couple of minutes later with a calendar. She sat down and looked through it and then said:

"I think the second weekend in March will work."

"That's better than the six or seven months I expected," Gail said and then she turned to me and asked, "How about it sugar; can you wait four months for me?"

"I can, but there is one thing that hasn't been discussed before now, and that is the fact that my mother will undoubtedly want to get involved."

"Just have her call me dear," Gail's mother said.

"I'll do better than that. Gail and I will take you and my parents out to dinner on Thursday. You need to get to know each other anyway."

"We would love to meet them," Gail's dad said.

I noticed Gail's face lose her smile when I said that I'd set up the dinner. Gail had already met my folks and had seemed to like them, so why the lost smile at my setting up a meeting of parents? And then it hit me. She had been planning on meeting one of her fuck buddies that evening. That thought wiped the smile off my face, but then I got a grip on myself. I'd known it was going to happen sooner or later and I had already agreed to look the other way.

When I left to go home Gal's goodnight kiss didn't lack the usual passion, so I guessed she didn't know that I'd caught her change of expression and figured out the cause. As I drove home I wondered for the hundredth time if I'd made a mistake. I didn't know any other guy who would accept what I had accepted, but I clung to the thought that if you wanted something bad enough, you had to be willing to pay the price.

\*\*\*

My parents and Gail's got along great and my mom and Gail's mom exchanged some ideas and arranged to get together several times over the coming weeks. My dad said:

"It is out of your hands now, Rob. All you have to do now is show up on time on the appointed day."

"That's not true," my mom said. "He has to pick out his best man and ushers and make up a list of who he wants invited. And the sooner the better."

I told her I'd get to work on it right away. Friday I called Mike and asked him to be my best man and he said he would, and then I called half a dozen good buddies and lined them up to be ushers and they all said yes. There were another dozen or so people I knew well enough and liked enough to invite and I made up the list and gave it to my mother on Friday. Then I picked Gail up and we headed for the cabin to spend a lazy weekend.

The next four months flew by. I was with Gail on the average of four times a week and I had no idea of what she did on the nights she wasn't with me and I made no attempt to find out. Gail had told me that she would do her absolute best to control her urges and I was hoping that she could do it.

I've mentioned Mike. But he wasn't the only buddy that I had. There were lots of others who, for the most part, did nothing to warrant mention in this tale. The same could not be said for some of Gail's friends. There were four in particular and all four had been Gail's friends since the second and third grades.

There was Bea whom I knew. Knew fairly well, as a matter of fact. Bea was one of the two girls who had dumped me for not having sex with her. There were the Fowler twins, Mary and Martha. They were fraternal and not identical.

And then there was Cindy.

Cindy was Gail's BFF and Cindy did not like me. She did not like me at all, and I had absolutely no idea why. I'd never met her before I started dating Gail and I could not remember ever saying anything to her or do anything to her that would give her the feelings she had toward me. Once she asked Gail right in front of me why she was wasting her time with a loser like me. Gail's response—"Because he's cute"—was less than satisfying to me at the time.

The nights that Gail wasn't with me, at least the ones she told me about, were invariably spent with the four on girl's nights out. Like it or not, the four were always going to be around even after Gail and I were married and all four were going to be a part of the wedding. Cindy was Maid of Honor and the other three were going to be bridesmaids.

***

The rundown to the wedding wasn't at all smooth. The thoughts that I had in my head about what Gail might be doing were being fed on occasion by guys that I knew.

One night Ray Hendrickson asked me if it didn't bother me some that Gail ran with a bunch of sluts. According to him the group never seemed to meet a cock they didn't like. He hastened to add that Gail didn't act like the rest of them; but did he say that because it was true or because he was my friend and didn't want to upset me?

Mike also made a comment or two about the group that Gail ran around with. Once, a month before the wedding, he asked me if I was sure that I knew what I was doing. When I asked him what he meant by that he said:

"It's like this. Say you absolutely love chocolate and one day someone gave you a whole case of Hershey Bars. You love chocolate so much that you sat down and ate the entire case in one sitting."

"What the fuck does that mean?"

"It means that just because you love something and really, really want it doesn't mean that it is good for you."

Before I could get him to clarify that for me he said he had to run and he got up and left. I'm not stupid and I knew what he was saying. He was flat out telling me in disguised fashion that he thought Gail wasn't good for me. Why did he think that? What did he know? Gail told me that she never did anything with anyone that I knew or did anything around people that knew us both. Was that true? Were Ray and Mike keeping something from me because they felt I'd turn away from them if they told me something they thought I wouldn't like or that would upset me greatly?

I fought hard to push those thoughts pout of my mind. I'd made my bed so to speak and I'd just have to lay in it. If Gail was doing what she said she would try her hardest not to do, I couldn't let it bother me. I'd said that I would go along with it and I would just have to.

***

Gail had her bachelorette party on the Tuesday before the wedding and I had my bachelor party on the Thursday before the wedding. It didn't have the usual stripper; just a lot of beer and card playing and before it was over, Mike made one last attempt.

"Are you really sure you want to do this Rob? You really want to tie yourself to a girl like Gail?"

"Why wouldn't I?"

"I'm going to be flat-assed honest with you bud, even at the risk of getting you pissed at me. I think the girl is a cock loving slut and I just can't see her being a faithful wife."

"Why would you think that?"

"I've heard rumors of what happened at her bachelorette party, and then of course there is the bunch she hangs out with."

"Just rumors?"

He looked away from me and said, "I know the male stripper Cindy hired for the party. He told me how wild things got. There were fourteen girls there and he had to call three friends to come and help him out. Things were so busy that he couldn't keep track of who did what, but he did say that at the end of his dance the bride to be sucked him off. By the way, he doesn't know you or that I know you."

"It changes nothing Mike. Probably a last sowing of wild oats before she settles into married life."

"It is your life bud, but I would be less of a friend if I didn't tell you what I know."

"Not to worry bro; I'll always owe you for pushing her into my arms."

\*\*\*

Two days before the wedding, Gail handed me the paperwork from a local lab that said she was disease free. She really didn't need to do it because the blood tests required to get the license were clear, but it is what I told her I had to have and she wanted to show me that she would keep her word.

The wedding went off as scheduled, but I was nervous and edgy most of the way through the ceremony. I half-expected someone to stand up and speak out when the good reverend got to the "Does anyone know of any reason that Robert and Gail should not be joined in Holy Matrimony"—but no one did it.

The reception was held at the VFW hall. It turned out that both my dad and Gail's dad were members. It was at the reception that I belatedly came to realize that Gail had had misled, if not outright lied, to me. She had told me that whatever she did wouldn't be with anyone I knew or around anybody who knew the both of us. It became obvious about an hour into the party when I noticed that the dates of Bea and Mary along with Martha's boyfriend and Cindy's fiancée Norm were throwing "knowing" smirks and grins my way. They knew! There was no doubt in my mind that they knew what Gail had been doing as had her four girlfriends. After I noticed I made damned sure that I sat with my back to them. It wasn't easy to totally ignore them since Cindy as Maid of Honor was always around and usually with her fiancé Norm.

About two hours into the party I needed to go outside for a breath of fresh air. No smoking rules either hadn't reached the VFW, didn't pertain to private clubs, or were just flat ignored and the smoke filled room had gotten to me.

I was sitting on a bench against the back wall of the building, and I was apparently under the partially opened women's bathroom window. I heard a couple of women come into the room talking to each other. I recognized the voices as belonging to Cindy and Mary.

"….here and part of it, but I still have a hard time believing that she married the twit," I heard Cindy say.

"I know. It doesn't make sense to me either. How someone with Gail's sexual appetites could marry a man without knowing if they are sexually compatible makes no sense at all."

"If I know my girlfriend as well as I think I do, she will be hanging horns on him if he doesn't toe the mark."

"Well she had better leave Tim alone because I plan on marrying him."

"You should have told her that before she tried him on. He seems to be around her a lot."

"Listen to yourself. You haven't been able to keep Norm out of her pants."

"What can I say? Friends share."

"She's going to let you fuck the twit?"

"Why the hell would I want to?"

"He's not a bad looking guy, and the fact that Gail won't tell us about his package leads me to believe he has something she doesn't want us to know about."

"So what? He is still a twit. I mean come on! I can see a seventeen year old or eighteen year old holding to a promise made to mommy, but a grown man who won't fuck because he promised mommy he wouldn't? Gail has to be nuts to have married him."

"Maybe, but then again maybe not. Maybe she thinks that if mommy can control him like that, she can too. You know the way he followed her around and mooned over her. She probably thinks she can get him to do whatever she wants."

"You might be right. Maybe she can pussy whip the twit into doing whatever she wants?"

"You think she can get him to watch while she fucks other guys? She has always liked fucking in front of us. The last time she did Norm she made sure that Tim, Ben and Sam sat and watched before inviting them in to make her airtight."

"Wouldn't surprise me a bit. I know how hung up she is on Norm's big dick. I doubt that she will give it up just because she is married now, and she will probably want to get the twit involved somewhere along the line so he won't nail her for cheating."

"Think you, me, Bea and Martha can work on her to turn him into a willing cuckold?"

"I'd be almost willing to be…" and they were gone.

But I was still there. Still there and wondering why the Fates and the Gods loved shitting on me. I sat there shaking my head as I came to grips with what I'd just heard. Mike had tried to warn me and so had Ray, but I of course knew better. They had to be wrong.

Shit! Who was I trying to kid. I'd known all along what Gail was doing even if I did pretend otherwise. But I wanted her so bad that I was willing to pay the price needed to get her; only, the price I had been expecting to pay was her occasionally meeting a guy not known to me to satisfy her need for sex. I knew it would stop as soon as I stepped up to take care of my husbandly duties. Now I had to ask myself if it would.

I might have still been a virgin, but that did not mean that I was ignorant when it came to things sexual. I'd seen plenty of porn and read erotic literature and I knew what 'airtight' meant. I was already asking myself if a girl who liked being that way was ever going to settle for being with just one man.

The other things I'd heard the two cunts talking about were also weighing on my mind. Was Gail with me because she expected to be able to control and manipulate me? I had to admit that the way I acted when I was around her might have given her the idea that she could do it. From the moment that I first set eyes on her I had behaved like a lovesick puppy whenever I was around her. Had she read something into that?

Another disturbing thought was that the two cunts thought they could get Gail to turn me into a willing cuckold. Could they do it? Could they convince Gail to try? They certainly knew her better than I did. They had insights into her character based on a relationship that went all the way back to grade school. Insights I couldn't begin to have.

Then there was the outright lying. Never with anyone I knew? Granted I didn't know them all that well, but I did know Norm, Tim, Sam and Ben. They were always around when Gail and I went to parties, barbecues and the like. Based on that lie I had to believe that she probably lied about never doing it where people who knew us both would see or be aware of what she was doing. I wondered how many people in attendance knew.

If I had any balls at all, I would get up, walk to my car, drive away and first thing Monday morning see an attorney about getting an annulment. The only problem was that I didn't have any balls where Gail was concerned.

I got up from my seat under the window and went back to the party. The first thing I saw when I walked back into the hall was the icing on the cake that the two cunts in the bathroom started baking in my mind—Norm was dancing with Gail. They were too close together to suit me and he had his hand on her ass. I may not have had the balls to walk away from Gail, but I did have balls and it was time to let some people know it. I walked up to Gail and Norm and keeping my voice low, but still full of menace I said:

"Get your fucking hands off of my wife's ass before I rip your arm off and shove it up your ass!"

His eyes got big and her let go of Gail and stepped back as I said:

"I'm cutting in and you would be wise to make yourself scarce."

"How dare you embarrass me like that?" Gail hissed at me.

"Where the fuck do you get off humiliating me in front of my friends and family by letting some asshole play with your ass in front of them?" I snarled right back at her.

Her eyes got big and the look on her face said as clear as day: *Whoa!! Where did that come from?* She had never had me speak to her before in that manner and in that tone of voice and it flat took her by surprise. She moved in close and buried her head into my chest like the new bride that she was and I wondered if we would have words on the way to the condo or after we got there. I didn't intend to carry it any farther if she dropped it, but she would get both barrels if she copped an attitude.

I had expected a glorious first night with my bride, but after what I'd heard and seen in the last hour, a ration of shit from Gail could damned well lead to an annulment attempt on Monday morning. Sooner if I could find an attorney open on Sunday.

She had eased my mind a bit when she whispered, "How much longer before we can get out of here? I want you baby. I've waited long enough. You've kept your promise and it's time."

"We can leave whenever you want. All the duty dances are done with and everyone knows that our flight to Aruba leaves early so it won't surprise anyone if we leave."

"Now. I want to leave now."

We made the rounds and said our goodbyes and then headed for home.

\*\*\*

Over the last couple of days we had gotten, Gail moved into the condo, so the condo was "home" for Gail now. She had of course been there many times, but I still performed the ritual "carry the new bride over the threshold" thing, and as I did it Gail said:

"Straight to the bedroom baby. No stops along the way."

Gail and I had never seen each other totally naked. I'd seen her naked from the waist down when I had eaten her pussy and she had seen me with my pants and briefs down to my knees when she had sucked my cock. We had seen each other in swimming suits and Gail in a bikini was an instant wood generator. I'd known that what I was getting was 'choice,' but even so, seeing her totally nude for the first time was breathtaking.

"Sit down on the bed baby," Gail said and so I did. She knelt in front of me and said, "I do not want our first time to be a quickie baby. I want it to last so I'm going to get the quick one out of the way."

She lowered her head and took my cock in her mouth. I looked down at her head bobbing up and down on me and all the bad thoughts I'd been having faded away. When I came she swallowed and stayed with it until I was limp and then she said:

"We need to get it back up baby," and she swung over me and positioned herself for our first sixty-nine. I knew what it took to get Gail off orally, but it took me a bit to figure out how to do it since we were basically upside down from the way I usually ate her. I did figure it out and I did get her off by the time she had me standing tall again.

I pushed her off me and onto her back and then moved between her legs. I was a virgin, but I knew what to do. I inserted Tab A into Slot B and Gail moaned:

"Yes, oh thank God yes."

Again, I was a virgin, but I knew what to do. Knowing of Gail's sexual nature, I was determined that she would never be able to find fault with me so I'd read and I studied and I'd watched a ton and a half of porn and I put it all to use. Slow and steady until she cried out for harder and faster, and then I took her to the edge and then backed off until she came back down from her orgasm and then I repeated things until I finally had to let go. It was a damned good first time, if I do say so myself.

I was lying there breathing hard and mentally patting myself on the back when I got my first real look at Gail's sexual nature. I was thinking that after an hour or two of rest we could try again, when Gail let me know there wasn't going to be an hour of two of rest. There wasn't even going to be five minutes.

She slid down, took my cock in her mouth and went to work at getting me up again, and of course she managed to get it done. Once she had me standing tall she introduced me to "cowgirl" and it did feel great, but after a while I came to realize I wasn't going to be able to get off that way. Gail got off three times before I had to roll her over onto her back and drive hard to get mine.

When I pulled out of her, I was thinking, "There! That ought to hold you for a while," but I was no sooner out of her than she had my cock in her mouth again. I couldn't let her just do me so I started to pull her into a sixty-nine and she pulled her mouth off me and said:

"Don't do that."

"Why not?"

"I'm full of your stuff."

"So what? You are sucking a cock that is coated in your stuff and mine."

"It's different baby. What is in me is in globs; what you have coating you is a thin layer."

"Don't care," I said as I tried to pull her on top of me.

"At least let me be on the bottom so it doesn't all flow out of me and onto your face."

I saw the wisdom in that and I rolled her into a sixty-nine with me on top. I would have bet a week's pay that she couldn't get me up again that night and I would have lost the bet. She did get me up and gave herself to me doggie and it took me a long time before I got off again. Gail was still trying to get me up again when I fell into an exhausted sleep.

\*\*\*

Our ten days in Aruba were spent sailing, scuba diving, hang gliding and making love. Three and four times a night, at least once in the morning and quite often a nooner. It was an absolutely glorious honeymoon, but sitting next to a snoozing Gail on the flight home the bad thoughts I had suppressed started sneaking back into my head.

I'd left Gail hanging a couple of times when she hadn't been able to get me to respond. I thought about her sexual appetites and I wondered if I was going to be enough for her. I remembered what Cindy and Mary had talked about in the bathroom and it of course bothered me. Especially the part about how much Gail liked to be airtight. If I couldn't answer the call when she needed me to, would she look to her fuck buddies to take up the slack? I hoped not because it would absolutely mean the end of our marriage.

We would no doubt socialize with Cindy, Mary, Martha and Bea and their men friends. The same men friends who Gail used to get herself airtight. Would they expect to be able to continue fucking her even though she was now married? Knowing how guys thought, I had no doubt that they would want to and would try, but would Gail go along?

I had to tell myself to trust her. She had been brutally honest with me before we got married and had emphatically stated more than once that she would not cheat on her man, but if I couldn't satisfy her sexually, would she change her stance on that?

*Hell of a way to start off your marriage Rob,* I was thinking on the way to the baggage claim area. *Not even married two full weeks and already wondering about your wife's fidelity.*

\*\*\*

We had returned on a Thursday and wouldn't be going back to work until Monday and Gail asked what I'd like to do over the weekend. I couldn't decide so she suggested a barbecue on Friday. March in

Colorado can be very springy weather wise, and it did look like it was going to be a nice weekend, so I said okay.

She invited a couple of her friends and I invited a couple of mine. Knowing that she was going to have Cindy, Mary, Martha and Bea (and no doubt their men friends), and remembering the overheard talk at the wedding reception, I ran to Radio Shack Friday morning and bought five voice activated digital recorders.

Paranoid? Probably, but as the old saying went, "Just because you think someone is out to get you doesn't mean that someone isn't." I put one in the bathroom, one in the kitchen, one in each of the two bedrooms and one in the living room. It might have been a complete waste of time and money, but if Cindy and her cohorts said anything, while at the condo; while near one of the recorders, I wanted to know what it was. I don't know who it was who said "Forewarned is forearmed," but whoever it was he had it right.

Everyone seemed to have a good time although there was one sour moment for me when I saw Gail off to the side of the patio talking to Norm. I remembered what I'd overheard while under that bathroom window, so seeing the two of them talking did bother me some, but I shook it off when they separated and Gail went over to talk to Mike. I was surprised when she went up on her toes and kissed his cheek and I wondered if I would ever know the story behind that.

The party started breaking up around ten, and as he was leaving Mike said the weather was nice enough for a round of golf and he asked if I would like to give it a shot on Saturday, and I told him Gail and I had a lunch date for Saturday so he suggested Sunday. I told him I would give him a call after checking with Gail to see if she had anything planned.

As soon as the last guest was gone, Gail dragged me into the bedroom and destroyed me. We slept in late, although when we did wake up she wanted to reenact the previous night; but she had to settle for a wake up and then once more when we showered together. She wanted to go back to bed for one more, but we were supposed to meet her parents and we would be more than fashionably late if we didn't get dressed and get a move on.

On the way to meet her parents I asked if she had plans for Sunday and she said:

"Just to stay in bed and wring you dry. Why?"

"Mike asked me to go out with him for a round of golf."

"As long as it isn't early in the morning. You need to understand something sugar. I intend to start all my weekends the same way we did this morning and that means that you are going to be bedroom busy until noon-ish on Saturdays and Sundays. I'm not sure that you will have enough left in you to chase after that silly white ball."

*** 

It turned out that there was an ulterior motive in Gail's parents inviting us to brunch. Mr. Luoma was in real estate and he asked me what I was going to do when my condo lease ran out in two months.

"Renew it, I suppose."

And then I got the lecture about building equity instead of collecting rent receipts. He knew of at least four houses that were on the market that would be just right for a couple starting out and if Gail and I were interested he would put up the down payment as a wedding present. I looked at Gail and she said:

"Makes sense to me, and we would eventually get a house anyway, so now is as good a time as any."

We didn't have anything else planned for the day and since Saturdays were prime showing days, we left the restaurant and followed Gail's dad and mom as he led us on a tour of the six homes he had mentioned. After the sixth, Gail asked me how I felt about the third one we had looked at.

"I liked it. I liked it a lot, but I'm afraid that it is just a bit out of my price range."

"Maybe it might be a little out of your price range, but it is not out of our price range. Don't forget sugar; when you married me you also married a second income."

We went back and took a closer look at the third house we had seen. It was a three bedroom ranch with a finished basement, an attached three car garage and a large patio area with a hot tub. The asking price was $229k, but Gail's dad said that it had been on the market for a while and we should offer $210k for it.

"They will probably say no to it, but offer to come down to $225. You counter with $215 and go back and forth and you can probably end up getting it for $220."

Gail and I drove home and talked it over. If the figures that Gail's dad gave us were right, the place would only cost two hundred a month more that the condo, so we decided to make an offer. Her dad's agency wasn't handling the property, but he told us who to contact and we decided to do it on Monday.

Taking Gail's warning to heart, I called Mike and told him I could hit the links with him as long as it was after twelve.

He laughed and said, "That's right. I forgot that you are a newlywed. I'll get us a tee time between twelve and twelve thirty."

Sunday morning was a repeat of Saturday morning, except we didn't have to stop at ten and go meet her parents. Gail was right when she said she wasn't sure I'd have enough energy to swing a club when she finished with me. I had one of my worst rounds ever.

Sitting at a table having a beer on the 19th Hole (that was actually the name of the clubs bar), Mike told me that he had a couple of reasons for wanting me to come out with him.

"The first of course is that I saw you watching when Gail kissed me at the barbecue and I just wanted you to know that it was entirely innocent. She thanked me for getting the two of you together and told me she would be in my debt for the rest of her life.

"The second reason is to give you a heads up on a possible problem. I was at a party last week and Cindy, her group of sluts and that bozo she hangs with, were there. Norm, right?"

I nodded a yes and he went on, "I overheard him bragging about doing Gail before you got married and he was willing to bet that he would be back in the saddle before you were married a month. I know that you guys had some sort of weird arrangement before you got married and I never understood it, but it seemed to work for you. There is no doubt in my mind that Gail is sold on you, but I felt that you needed to be aware of the snakes that are crawling around in the bushes."

"I appreciate the warning. It isn't the first I've heard of it and you can bet that I'll be keeping my eyes open."

***

When I got home there was a note on the kitchen table that Gail had gone grocery shopping. I thought I might have time to check the recorders so I gathered them all up and sat down at the kitchen table to listen to them. I had labeled them using masking tape so I'd know which one had been where.

There was nothing of interest on the ones from the bedrooms and living room, but there was stuff on the bathroom and kitchen recorders. I had to wade through a lot of stuff before getting to the nitty-gritty. The kitchen window looks out onto the patio and Norm and Tim must have been there looking out the window at the people on the patio. I heard Tim say:

"She sure is looking sexy today. Think we will ever fuck her again?"

"I'd bet on it," Norm said. "Any broad who loves threesomes and foursomes as much as Gail does isn't going to settle for just one cock even if it is her husband's. I bet Marv Pallister twenty bucks that I'd be fucking her before she is married a month."

"How you going to do that?"

"She will still hang with Cindy so there will be plenty of opportunities."

"If you do get her, I want in on it."

"Not to worry my man. She is going to want those threesomes and foursomes again and we already know that Cindy will help us make it happen."

Someone else came into the room and the two stopped talking, and if they picked it up again it was somewhere not covered by a recorder. The bathroom recorder had three sections that I found interesting. The first was of Gail and Cindy. Can anyone tell me why women have to go to the bathroom in pairs? Anyway, between the sounds of peeing, hand washing and the like, Cindy said:

"Norm wants to know how long he has to wait before he can play with you again. The rest of the guys would like to know also."

"Norm and the guys are going to have to settle for you, Bea and the twins. I've got my man now and I'm not going to do anything that might make me lose him."

"Oh come on girlfriend. There is no way that a girl who loves sex as much as you do can settle for just one cock. Don't forget, sweetie, that I've seen you doing three at a time and absolutely loving it."

"That was then, but this is now, and I've got Rob and he is all I need."

"Yeah! Like I'm going to believe that."

The toilet flushed and the two left the room. The next snippet of interest was a conversation between Bea and Mary. Bea said:

"This is a fun party." Mary answered, "Not much fun for me. All the cocks are covered up. How long do you think it will be before Gail gets her doofus husband loosened up enough that we can get back to doing some real partying?"

"According to what Cindy just told me, it will probably be never."

"Never on doofus or on partying again?"

"According to Cindy, Gail says she intends to remain true. Why do you keep calling him doofus? He seems like a pretty nice guy."

"Because he is breaking up our group. It isn't going to seem right getting down without Gail. Your turn," followed by the sounds of flushing. Then Mary said:

"Cindy says she will get Gail back into the swing of things even if she has to drug Gail or the doofus."

"What the hell does that mean?"

"I don't know. Drug doofus and take pictures of him with a cock up his ass or down his throat while he is out of it and show Gail the photos. Maybe drug Gail and take pictures of her doing what she does best and show the pictures to doofus. How do you think doofus would react to seeing his bride three-holed?"

"I can't believe Cindy would stoop that low."

"What can I say? She flat does not like doofus and she would be tickled to death to break the two of them up."

Then there was the sound of flushing and the two of them left.

The next interesting piece was Bea and Martha talking. The conversation must have started on the way to the bathroom so I didn't hear the first part of it.

".....think I should do about it," Bea asked.

"Don't ask me. I'm somewhat on Cindy's side. It just isn't the same without Gail. On the other hand, Gail seems super happy to be with Rob and I wouldn't want to be part of messing that up for her."

"But Gail and Cindy have been best friends since the second grade so would she even believe me if I warned her? Or would she shoot the messenger? I don't want to lose her friendship. We have been friends since grade school and that means something to me."

"If you feel that strongly about it, you have to do something."

"But what?"

"I don't know. Maybe instead of telling Gail you should tell Rob. Warn him and let him handle it, but if you decide to go that way you had better do it in a hurry. Cin says she is going to talk Gail into having a girls night out every two weeks or so and if Gail agrees it is likely that whatever she plans on doing will happen on one of those nights."

The sounds of flushing and hand washing followed by, "I just don't know…" and they were gone.

I copied the kitchen and bathroom sections and had just finished when Gail got home.  I got a big kiss and she said:

"I've got a couple more of those for you if you will help me bring the groceries in."

I did get a couple more and they lead us into the bedroom where Gail did her best to destroy me.

*** 

The next morning on the way to work I decided that I needed a tap on the home phone.  I stopped at Radio Shack and bought another recorder, and the clerk told me where I could go on the Internet to get directions on how to put in a tap.

I left work early that afternoon and stopped by the agency that was handling the house that Gail and I had decided on.  I made the $210k offer and then headed on home.  I got on my desktop and went searching and by the time Gail got home I had the tap in place.  I didn't do it because I didn't trust Gail (at least I told myself that) but because I wanted to know about any plans that Cindy might try and make with her.

The usual *Forewarned is forearmed* thing.

The home tap might not be any help because Cindy could call Gail at work or on her cell phone to make plans.  From what I'd learned so far, it seemed very likely that whatever Cindy planned on doing would happen when she and Gail were out together and I wanted as much of a heads up as I could get.

The next ten days were filled with work and the nights were filled with Gail doing her best to collect my life insurance although I wasn't sure that the policy would pay off because of my being fucked to death.  They might consider that a form of suicide and refuse to pay.

The same ten days saw offers and counter offers and in the end Gail's dad put up the down payment on the house we agreed to pay $217k for. Closing was to be in thirty days, but we could move in right away and pay rent until closing.

We were not even moved in yet and Gail was already planning the house warming party. I was visualizing the place and trying to decide where to put the recorders.

# Chapter 3

Four days before we moved into the house, Gail asked me if I would mind if she had a girl's night out after work with Cindy, Bea and the twins. It didn't surprise me because I knew it was coming after listening to the bathroom conversations and I'd heard Cindy bring it up on yesterday's output from the phone tap. Gail said that she would think about it and let Cindy know after running it by me.

I gambled on Cindy not rushing into her plans and taking the time to set things up so I told Gail I was okay with her having a night out with the girls.

"The girls Gail; not the girls *and* the boys."

She gave me a funny look, but didn't say anything.

The next night was her G.N.O. and she was home by eight and I breathed a little easier knowing that there hadn't been enough time between Gail's five-thirty quitting time at work and the time she got home for anything to have happened.

The next three days were spent moving into the new house and by Tuesday evening we were in the home. Gail was all for having her housewarming party on the coming weekend, but I thought we should wait until after closing and the house was actually ours. She pouted and so I gave in. In a way it was a good thing because if we had waited until after closing it would be at least thirty days during which Cindy might get around to doing something.

I didn't know if my phone tap and recorders would give me anything, but I had to hope. I hit Radio Shack and got five more recorders and by the time the guests started arriving for the party, I had the living room, kitchen, all three bathroom and bedrooms, the finished basement, the garage and the hot tub covered with recorders.

It was a fun party and I had a good time even though I did have to spend some of it keeping an eye on Cindy and her herd, which consisted of the usual group of four and their men friends, which wasn't all that hard since the gas grill I was manning was positioned so everything was in front of me.

I saw Norm get Gail off to the side three times. The first time he talked to her for several minutes and I saw her shake her head no before walking away from him. Half an hour later he got her off to the side again and talked for several minutes before leaning forward and saying something in her ear. She pushed him away and walked away from him. The third time after a couple of minutes talking she slapped his face hard and walked away. I of course acted like I'd not seen a thing.

When the invitations had gone out, the invitees were told to bring swimming suits in case they wanted to try out the hot tub. Several times during the party I saw Cindy and several of her cohorts in the tub soaking, and toward the end of the party I saw Gail, Cindy and Mary soaking and talking. I didn't know if I would get anything from the rest of the recorders, but I was betting that I'd get a ton of stuff off the one hidden by the hot tub. Hopefully some of it would be useful to me.

The party started breaking up around ten and by eleven all the guests were gone. Gail said to leave the cleanup for the next day and she drug me off to bed and worked me until I passed out from exhaustion. She let me sleep in until nine the next morning and then woke me up with a blow job that led to a session of doggie followed by a shower. We had a simple breakfast of cereal and toast and then got to work cleaning up the mess.

Around one Gail went over to her parents' house and that gave me a chance to gather up all the recorders. There was nothing of interest on the living room or bedroom recorders (there was some on the master bedroom recorder, but it was just me and Gail going at it).

The garage had an interesting segment. It recorded Norm fucking Mary on the hood of one of the vehicles. I couldn't tell from the recorder if it was my truck or Gail's car.

There was some on the kitchen recorder. The kitchen overlooked the patio, the same as the kitchen window in the condo had, and the recorder picked up Norm, Ted and Jake talking. They were watching Gail circulate among the guests and Norm was saying:

"I'm gonna fuck her and make her beg me to keep fucking her."

"Let me know when it happens," Jake said. "I want more of that tight ass myself."

"I don't know guys," Ted said. "I think if she was going to cut loose she would have done it by now. She could never go three or four days without being three-holed before she married Rob, and it's been what, five or six weeks now?"

Someone came into the kitchen and the three apparently dispersed.

I was surprised that I didn't get anything on the bathroom recorders, but the hot tub recorder made up for it. The first was Cindy, Mary and Martha.

"You still planning on setting Gail up on one of our nights out?" Mary asked.

"I don't know yet. I'm still trying to make up my mind on whether to set Gail up, set Rob up or do them both. I'm leaning toward both. Rob is so gaga over Gail that he might just forgive her. I don't think Gail would forgive him if she caught him. If I do them both and she goes off on him hard enough, it might make him pull back from her."

The talking stopped when a couple more people got in the tub.

The next piece of interest was Cindy talking to Norm.

"I saw Gail slap you. What was that all about?"

"I tried to get her to go into the house with me and give me a blow job or let me fuck her from behind while she leaned forward on the kitchen table and watched doofus flip burgers."

"I told you to stay away from her. I don't need you making her leery of being around us. We will get her back in the group, but it will take a little time to set it up. Have you found anybody you can get GHB from yet?"

"No, but I found a guy who can get us knockout drops. When are we going to do it?"

"We can't do anything until we come up with some sort of date rape drug."

"I've got some feelers out. Once I get the stuff, what is the plan?"

"Give Gail the drug and once she gets going, take pictures and see to it that they get to Rob."

"What about him?"

"Give him the knockout drops and while he is out, pose him in some pictures so that it looks like he is having a good time and then see to it that Gail finds the pictures."

"Made up your mind yet as to whether it will be with a male or female?"

"Why? You want to do him in the ass? Or maybe stick your dick in his mouth?"

"It would be a kick to fuck both Gail and her hubby."

"You stop to think how she might take it to see you doing her beloved? You might never get a taste of her again."

The conversation ended as someone got into the tub with them.

Next up it was Bea, Mary and Martha.

"You think Cindy's plan will work?" Martha asked.

"Should," Mary answered. "I don't know about the Rob part though. I think she is going a little overboard on the guy thing. I think it would work better if Gail saw pictures of him with another girl."

"Who could we get to do it?"

"I'd do it," Mary said. "I'd like to see what he's got that has Gail so sold on him."

Martha said, "Get real Sis. If she saw you with him she wouldn't have any more to do with you. The object here is to get her back into the group; not split it up farther."

"I'd tell her that I did it for her. Tell her I had to show her what a cheating asshole he was before she got too deep into her marriage to him."

"Think she would buy it?"

"Of course she would. We have been friends forever and she would know I wouldn't lie to her."

Just then Cindy and Gail joined them in the tub. Cindy asked, "How about Tuesday night for our next girl's night out? That okay with you guys?"

"Count me in," Bea said.

"Me too," Mary said.

"Why not. Works for me," Martha said.

"How about you girlfriend?" Cindy asked Gail.

"Tuesday should be good for me, but I'll tell you again what I told you the last time. It is a girl's night out only. If I show up and find any of the guys there I'll turn around and leave, and if any of them show up I'll get up and leave."

"You're no fun."

"I told all of you that when I got married there would be no more Gail the Wild Child. I meant it. I will not do anything that will get between me and my honey."

"What the hell does he have that makes him so special?" Mary asked.

"It isn't so much what he's got, but what I have."

"What's that?"

"Love girlfriend. Deep abiding love."

The conversation ended there as Gail's mom and dad joined them in the tub.

It gave me a lot to think about. I had originally believed that all of what Cindy was saying was just talk, but I was beginning to take what she was saying seriously. The question of course was: *What the fuck are you going to do about it Rob?*

With what I knew about Gail, there was no doubt in my mind that if they got her going again, she would keep on going. It would be a case of her thinking, "Oh well; I tried, but the horse is out of the barn now. I don't dare let Rob see the pictures. I hid it from him before we got married and I can hide it from him now." Not showing much faith in my bride I suppose, but knowing what I knew about what she did before we were married, what else was I to think?

Granted that she was upfront with me about her "needs"; but even though she was upfront, she still shaded the truth and intentionally misled me with the "No one you know" and "Never around anyone who knows us both" bullshit. I was willing to pay the price I needed to pay to get her, but was I willing to pay the same price to *keep* her? I knew the answer to that in a flash.

Hell no!!!

She said "I do" to the "Forsaking all others" part of the wedding ceremony—I was damned well going to hold her to it. The question facing me was "Do I go proactive or do I wait and see?" I made the decision that proactive was the way I was going to go.

It took me a day to get things together, and Wednesday after dinner I told Gail that we needed to talk.

"About what?"

"Several things, but mainly about your friendship with Cindy, Bea, Mary and Martha."

"Is this about the way Cindy behaves toward you?"

"In a way, I guess that is part of it. Her dislike of me probably has a lot to do with it. It is going to take me some time to get it all out and I would appreciate your not interrupting me until I'm done."

I told her what I'd overheard while sitting under the bathroom window and how that had made me put recorders around the condo.

"You might recall the mood I was in when I came in from hearing what I heard and found you dancing with Norm's hand on your ass. First off, I'm not pleased with the way you misled me or outright lied to me about not doing anything with anyone I knew or not doing it around anyone who knew us both. The bottom line is that your friends are not mine and your friends have an agenda that, if successful, will ruin your marriage.

"I am not going to tell you what your friends are saying and then go through the "They wouldn't say that" or the "You must have misunderstood them" bull crap. I have put it all on this recorder and you can listen to it at your leisure."

I put the recorder down on the table in front of her and said, "The first part is what was recorded at the condo and the second part is what was recorded at our barbecue. I want you to listen to the recorder and hear in their own words what your friends have planned for us. I'm going to run down to the bar and have a beer or two while you listen. When I get back we can discuss it."

I got up and left her sitting at the kitchen table staring down at the recorder in front of her.

***

Harry Short and Dick Moore were at the bar when I got there and I drank beer and shot pool with them for a couple of hours and then I headed back home. Gail wasn't there so I went up to bed and sacked out.

I didn't hear Gail when she came in, but I woke up in the morning with her snuggled up next to me. She must have been awake because when I stirred her hand found my cock and she started fondling it. As usual, when she paid attention to my dick it got hard, and when it got hard she just had to make it go soft again. She accomplished that and I got up to shower only to have her follow me in which led to more hardening and softening.

It was a work day so we didn't take it back to the bed. As it was, we didn't get to the gym until almost six-fifteen. The subject of Cindy and the other three wasn't brought up and I was going to let Gail be the one to start that conversation. She did it when we into the hot tub after our workout.

"I listened to the recorder and at first I didn't believe that it was anything but talk. Cindy was upset over me taking myself out of the group so I thought it was just sour grapes on her part. In my mind I was all set to dismiss what I'd heard until it got to the part recorded here at the house. I played it twice before I accepted that Cindy might really be planning on doing something.

"I got the feeling listening to Bea's part that she really wasn't on board with the plan and was looking for some way to let me know what was going on, so I took the recorded and went over to see her. She apologized for not coming forward, but she was torn between her feelings for the other girls and me. She felt she would lose me as a friend if she said nothing and would lose the others if she warned me.

"She confirmed that it was all true and that Cindy had already set a time for it to happen. She expects us to have more barbecues now that we are in the house and her plan is to make her move at the next one. She is going with the two part plan. Knockout drops for you and date rape drugs for me. She expects that once she gets me started that I will go back to what she believes is my true persona, which she believes is sex-crazed cock-loving slut.

"I swore Bea to secrecy about my visit with her and told her that none of the group would ever hear from me what we had talked about. I'm not all that happy with Cindy, and I plan on doing something that will let her know it. Can I count on you to help?"

"Knowing what she had planned for me? You bet your sweet little perfect ass I'll help. What do you have in mind?"

"Do to them what they were going to do to us."

"How is that getting back at Cindy? She would love it just like she thinks you would."

"Cindy is a bigot. She calls Afro-Americans mud people and worse. Just imagine her seeing a video of herself with a couple of black guys. As for manly man Norm, just think of what a few pictures floating around of him with a guy buried in his butt and a cock in his mouth would do to him."

"I don't give a rat's ass in Norm's case, but could you really do that to your best friend forever?"

"She lost her best friend status when I married you. You are my best everything now. She dropped to second place on the list when I got you, but even so I have to ask myself just how good of a friend she really is if she was going to do to me what she had planned."

"How do you see it happening?"

"We will invite Cindy and Norm over for dinner some evening and do it then. Your part will be to find the guys who will do the deed. You have black friends and gay friends and I'm hoping that you know some of them well enough to ask them for a teensy-tiny favor. Tell them that their faces won't show in any of the pictures. I'll handle getting the date rape drug and knockout drops."

"You sure you want to do this?"

"My so-called best friend wanting to fuck up the best thing that ever happened to me? Damned straight I want to do it."

\*\*\*

And so on the first Saturday in May, Cindy and Norm showed up for the dinner we had invited them to. They were surprised to find out that they weren't the only ones invited. There was Jason Mars along with

Jefferson English and also in attendance were Gary Morris and Jerome Appleton. It was interesting to watch Cindy when she was introduced to Jason and Jeff since they were both black, but she hid her racist tendencies well. Cindy and Norm no doubt noted how "touchy-feely" Gary and Jerome were, which was not surprising since they were an openly gay couple.

The evening went surprisingly well, and around nine-thirty Gary and Jerome said they needed to get going since they had an early tee time the next morning. Jason was the next to go and shortly thereafter Jeff also left. Gail asked Cindy and Norm to hang around for a little longer and I poured a generous amount of Baileys Irish Cream in four glasses and we went into the living room and settled into the couch and easy chairs.

Gail proposed a toast to "Good friends" and then said, "I have something I need you to hear."

She placed a recorder on the coffee table and hit "play," and Cindy and Norm got to listen to the same recordings that Gail had listened to the night I had confronted her about her friendship with Cindy and the others. Cindy and Norm sat there and squirmed as they looked everywhere but at Gail or me. When the recorder went silent, except for a low hiss Gail said:

"I have one more recording for you to listen to," and she put a second recorder on the table and hit play. We had taken a second recorder and had reenacted our conversation where Gail had outlined her plan for them. As they listened their eyes got big as it dawned on them what the other four males in attendance could have done to them had we followed through on Gail's plan.

When the recording ended Gail said, "You can thank soft-hearted Rob for us not putting the plan into actual play. He seemed to think that regardless of what you were going to do, a sixteen year-old friendship was worth trying to hold onto. All I can say to that is that we will see.

"For now I think we should call it a night."

I nursed my Baileys while Gail walked them out.

*** 

Two days later on Monday Gail met with Bea, Mary and Martha and played both recordings for them. Bea had already heard the first one, but had to sit through it again because Gail didn't want the others to know she had talked with Bea.

Gail didn't tell me the outcome of that meeting and I didn't ask, but the following Tuesday Gail did go out for a night with her four friends. But before that night out I got a surprise visit. I'd just gotten back from lunch when my secretary told me that there was a Cindy Martin there wishing to speak with me. I told her to send Cindy in.

I rose to meet her and offered her a seat and then sat back down.

"Surprised?" she asked.

"That's putting it mildly."

"I don't know if it is even possible, but I am here to try and mend fences. What you did was a wake-up call for me."

"What I did for you?"

"Not letting Gail's plan happen."

"And it woke you up how?"

"I wasn't thinking of Gail when I was doing my plotting. I was only thinking of me. I didn't give a thought to Gail's happiness. I was only thinking of mine. Our little group has been together for over sixteen years and you were doing something that no one else had ever done. You were splitting us up. No guy had ever done that before. Guys came and went but none of them ever threatened the group until you came along. It was driving me crazy. I couldn't let the group—my extended family—break up.

"You had to be stopped. I knew that once I got you out of the way Gail would be back with us. Again, I was thinking of what *I* wanted and not thinking about anyone else. I know Gail cares for me. I know she would take a bullet for me if it came to that, just as I would for her. We were that tight. That she would do what she planned told me just how serious she was where you were concerned. I'm not sure that our friendship would have survived that and that friendship is precious to me.

"You had every reason to want to hurt me and yet you would not let her do it, so I owe you big time, and my paying the debt off starts with me crawling to you, telling you that I'm sorry for what I've done and beg you for forgiveness."

It was a much different Cindy who left my office that afternoon. Our relationship wasn't suddenly sunshine and roses, but it did get better over time. It even got to the point where we hugged each other and kissed each other on the cheek.

\*\*\*

Gail's friendship with the four continued, although what Cindy feared did happen to a degree. The group never actually split up, but changes did happen. Cindy dumped Norm and after going through a couple of other boyfriends, she now has a ring on her finger and a date set for a wedding.

Bea met and married a guy she met at a seminar that her employer sent her to. They have twin girls and Bea is expecting again.

Next to go was Martha. She got hooked by a blind date that Mary had set her up with.

Mary is still a cock-crazy slut and she makes no bones about it. "I love variety too much to ever pick one man and marry him. I'd be cheating on the poor guy inside of a month. Why do that to both of us when I can just stay single and do my think."

Mike is Mary's counterpart, although for the last eight months he has been keeping company with the same girl, which is six months longer than he stayed with any other lady.

Once everyone knew about the recorders there was no sense in keeping them in play, so I gathered them up and donated them to Goodwill.

For the first two years of our marriage Gail did her best to reduce me to a smoking ruin, but motherhood changed that. I've been told that pregnancy makes women even hornier, but it seemed to do the opposite to Gail. She was still hot as hell, but didn't seem to want or need it as much as she had before she got pregnant, and her needs and wants didn't pick back up after Billy was born.

He was followed by Charlie and Mary Beth and we decided that we had a big enough family and I got myself snipped. Gail still wants it four or five times a week, but rarely do we have any more all-nighters or Saturdays and Sundays from wakeup until noon.

I look at where we are today and what we have in each other, and I'm damned sure that I did the right thing when I paid the price I had to pay to make Gail my bride.

## -The End-

Here is a sample from another story you may enjoy:

# SWEET REVENGE

SEXY EROTICA

## Just Plain Bob

I picked her up at the apartment that she shared with two other girls and we went out for dinner, drinks and dancing. She seemed a little nervous when she got into the car and I put it down to the fact that this was the first time I had picked her up instead of meeting her some place. I got the feeling from the way she was acting that she was afraid of being seen with me and I asked her about it as I pulled away from the curb.

"It's my dad. He has been asking Gwen and Harriet (her roommates) about what I've been doing and who I've been seeing. Gwen even told me that he is paying part of her rent to keep an eye on me. If he's paying Gwen, he is probably paying Harriet also."

"Why would he do something like that?"

"He worries about me doing something stupid and ruining my life. He never wanted me to move out of the dorms in the first place."

"What have you done to make him think that you are going to do something stupid?"

"It isn't what I've done, but what my two sisters have done."

"And what is that?"

"They dropped out of school and got married to guys whom my dad considers fortune hunters. He says that Amos and Jack only married my sisters because of their trust funds."

"Trust funds?"

"My grandparents set up trust funds for all three of us grandchildren."

"You have a trust fund? We have been dating over two months now so how come I've never heard of it?"

"I think dad is right about Amos and Jack so I don't tell guys about it because I want to be sure they want me and not the two million I'll get when I either graduate from college or get married."

"So what you are saying is that if your dad finds out about me, he will assume that I'm just another fortune hunter? Is that why I've never met your parents?"

"Yes to both."

"Well I can put your mind and your dad's mind to rest. If our relationship gets to the point where I ask you to marry me, and I don't mind saying that it is extremely likely that I will, I will sign a prenuptial agreement that will satisfy your father."

"You would do that?"

"Sure I would. I don't need your money. I have a trust fund of my own that I get when I turn thirty. It is only half as big as yours, but it is enough."

"I never knew that."

"My dad clued me in real early about women who would come after me for the money so like you I've always kept quiet about it. I think that we are far enough along in our relationship to realize that neither of us is after the other for their money."

"I still don't want my dad to know about us. Because of what my sister's did he will try and split us apart."

"Ain't gonna happen, kiddo, it just ain't gonna happen."

We had dinner at Duke's Steak House and then went to the Black Onion for drinks and dancing. We had been there about an hour and I'd had two drinks and Connie had consumed four as we danced and enjoyed ourselves when my cell rang. I answered it and then told Connie that it was a call that I had to take and I got up and went to find some quiet.

I went into the men's room and found Charlie waiting for me. "Ready?" I asked and he smiled and said, "We're good to go. See you in a few," and he left the room. I went into one of the stalls and sat down. I took the crossword puzzle that I'd clipped out of the daily paper out of my pocket and began to work it. It took me twelve minutes which I figured was enough time.

I headed back to my table and when I got there I saw Charlie and Connie out on the dance floor. I sat down at the table and waited. When the music stopped, they came back to the table and Charlie scowled when he saw me.

"This is a private party, bud. Scram!"

"It is indeed a private party and I don't recall inviting you. Did you invite him, Connie?"

"No, but he was kind of pushy and it was easier to dance with him than cause a scene."

"Hey! I bought you two drinks."

"And it got you three dances, which were more than you had any right to expect."

If you enjoyed this sample then look for <u>Sweet Revenge</u>.

**Also by this Author:**

The Prodigal Family: The Abbotts

Watching My Shared Wife

The Waitress and the Runaway Husband

Baiting Mr. Little

Too Hot for Henry

Chuck's Fantasy

The Redhead's Desires

Rescued at Riley's

His Every Fantasy

Open Mike Night

Pursuit for Revenge

Why Does He Do That?

Halloween & Drugs

Tracey

When Rob Met Kari

Becoming a Shared Wife, Vol. 1 –
(Wife Sharing and Other Adventures)

Becoming a Shared Wife, Vol. 2 –
(Hazardous Wives)

Becoming a Shared Wife, Vol. 3 –
(Wives Who Stray)

## From the Author

## WANT FREE COPIES OF MY BOOKS?
Just visit my blog and download free copies of my books:
**awesomeauthors.org/justplainbob**

Yes, I write about sluts and whores because as everyone knows, you tend to write about the things you know. And I do like sluts and whores, just not the ones that lie to me and cheat on me.

So be forewarned - if you click on a Just Plain Bob story you will be getting sluts, whores and husbands who do not kill, maim and destroy. There are other things you will rarely find in a Just Plain Bob story.

If you enjoyed any of my books then please share the love and promote my books in Amazon. I would really appreciate your honest reviews, too!

Good news is always welcome.

One Last Thing, For Kindle Readers...

When you turn the page, Kindle will give you the opportunity to rate this book and share your thoughts on Facebook and Twitter. If you enjoyed my writings, would you please take a few seconds to let your friends know about it? Because... when they enjoy they will be grateful to you and so will I.

Thank you!

**Just Plain Bob**
justplainbob@awesomeauthors.org

**You may also like the books by these authors:**

# Hot Erotica
## George X. Bush

# DESIRED
## by the Boys

### IN THE CABIN

Mary was fed up with being left behind each month while Riley went up to the cabin with his three friends, Mark, Robert, and John, to fish, drink and just have fun. She was only 23 and she wanted some fun, too. She resented being left behind to fend for herself in this way. She poured herself another drink, her third, and flopped down onto the sofa in frustration as she sipped her drink. *I'll show him*, she thought, sipping her drink, a plan coming into her head. Quickly gulping the rest of her drink down, Mary went to her room and quickly threw a change of clothes and some toiletries into a bag, grabbing her pocketbook and keys as she locked the door behind her and got into the car. If she drove steadily, she could be there in three hours and surprise them.

Mary had to stop a couple of times on the way as she felt herself getting tired, but she finally pulled up to the cabin around four in the morning. As she let herself in, she heard the sounds of snoring coming from different areas of the cabin. She was tired and felt a bit ragged from all she had drunk during the evening, so she quietly tiptoed to the bathroom to take a shower. The water felt so good after the long drive and she stood under it enjoying the sensation.

When she got out of the shower and dried herself, she appraised what she was seeing in the mirror. Her long red hair hung down to the middle of her back. She had that pale skin with light freckles that was common to redheads. Her breasts were very full with large pale nipples on the ends. Mary cupped them in her hands, gently squeezing them as her fingers automatically sought out and found her nipples, squeezing them and pinching them, pulling on them as they screwed themselves into large hard knots. Her hands trailed down her flat stomach to where a small thatch of bright red pubic hair used to grow above her pussy. She had no hair on her pussy, having had it removed by electrolysis so that it was as smooth as a baby's. At the top of her slit, her clit hood peeked through her pussy lips and her clit, fat as a pinkie finger, stuck out from beneath its hood. Her hand trailed down and her fingers trailed up through and between her pussy lips, feeling herself and the wetness that was starting. Her legs were long and straight, as were her feet and toes. Men had always found her beautiful and at the moment she quite agreed with them.

She was still squeezing her breasts with one hand, her other still between her legs when suddenly the door opened and Robert staggered in, completely naked, his cock dangling in front of him, bigger than anything Mary had ever imagined. As he shut the door, he blinked his eyes, trying to clear the fog of alcohol and sleep so he could make sense of what he was seeing.

"Mary?" he croaked, his voice still sounding a bit drunk.

"Hi, Robert," Mary said, frozen where she stood, her hands not moving.

"What're you doin' here?" he asked, slurring his words. "And how come you're naked?"

"Uh, I thought I'd drive up and surprise Riley and I just took a shower," she replied, letting her hands fall to her sides as she stared at his cock which was beginning to grow even larger...

If you enjoyed this sample then look for **Desired By The Boys**.

# ABBY
## CITY GIRL IN THE COUNTRY
### Erotic Romance

# KERRY JAMES

Abby had little difficulty in getting to this point, on the B3227 from Taunton heading towards South Molton, and guessed that somewhere on this road she should see a sign indicating her turn. Yet as she drove further and further into Devon she became uneasy that no such sign had revealed itself. Navigation became more of a problem as she drove deeper into the countryside, signposts, when you could find them; indicated a destination which then received no further mention at all upon succeeding signs. High banks on either side of the road meant that she had little clue as to where she was, the only point of reference was the ribbon of road unwinding ceaselessly and vanishing under the bonnet of her car and the occasional signs for some oddly named village or hamlet. As she passed through villages such as Wiveliscombe and Bampton, she wondered if she had gone wrong, and seeing the sign that said South Molton was just five miles farther on, decided that indeed she had gone wrong. Swearing mildly under her breath, Abby was giving thought to turning round and retracing her path.

Suddenly, she caught that breath; there was the sign. Leaning gently against the high banks that enclosed the road with a vigorous growth of Ivy as camouflage, she would have missed it had she not been driving slowly looking for a place to turn. It was a peculiar sensation, and her heart was beating furiously as she made the turn. A name that had previously existed only in hearsay and on a map was now a fact. Her mother had mentioned the name a few times without thinking, but would not be pressed on its significance. When her mother had died, Abby was nineteen, there was no reference at all to the name in her personal effects, which were few, there was no birth certificate, and the only official document she could find was an out of date passport, giving the birth area as South Molton. Abby's history consisted of just her mother's death certificates, and her own birth certificate. Abby now realised that she could have obtained a copy of her mother's birth certificate, but as is the way of things she had not thought logically at the time. She would repair this oversight as soon as possible. She wondered why her mum had a passport, as she had never travelled abroad.

Combe Linney, as Abby spelt it, was not even marked on her road map, and she had to resort to the Ordinance Survey to discover the location; again there was no place spelt Linney, but there was a Combe Lyney, near South Molton, and she assumed that this had to be the place. Its sum total consisted of two black oblongs, and a round dot with a cross on top, presumably indicating a church. There were no A or B roads that ventured anywhere near the place. If this wasn't the back of beyond, then it was pretty close to it.

The mystery could not be investigated immediately as Abby had after her mother's death, to consider the business of life, a job, somewhere to live. Her mother had left her little, but a stubborn trait that helped Abby survive the numerous jobs she took in the financial and insurance trade; making tea and coffee for surly men and women who viewed her simply as the office gofer.; They would have been surprised if they had known that Abby did not merely put their drinks in front of them, but closely studied what they were doing. They didn't know because Abby was invisible, unimportant, not even missed when she left to go to a better job, using all she had learned to pack her C.V. She was twenty-five when she started in the city as a proprietary equity trader, the years of watching and learning placed her in good stead. She would not say that she was a brilliant trader, there were many more that could turn sixpences into sovereigns at the drop of a hat, but she was intuitive, and with no family to call upon her time, was content to work all hours to achieve her goal. In a business where employers counted the hours almost as important as the success, she was regarded highly.

If you enjoyed this sample then look for <u>Abby</u>.

G. Stuart Crane

# THE FLOG ZONE

## PARANORMAL PRECOGNITION

# BDSM Erotic Romance

John Peters didn't know what his first birth was like, but his second one was agonizing. He remembered the pain, the drowsy driver crossing lanes, the sounds of crushing and crumpling metal and glass, the fire, and the screaming of his lungs out as they were seared by the very air he breathed. This passed and he felt a new sensation of someone using his/her hands to move his legs. Then came the hot kiss of a lash, and he felt as if he were being flogged forever when he tried to open his eyes to scream. Then the pain turned to pleasure and as it continued till the lash fell.

The scream came out as a gurgle, a whisper. His eyes opened to see light blue walls all around him and that he was in a bed. A woman in surgical scrubs was moving his legs and feet, stretching them, moving them back and forth at the ankles and knees. The woman was pleasant, not pretty in the formless clothes she wore, but with her red hair back in a short ponytail. Expressive green eyes is now wide and watching him. She had stopped what she was doing and was watching a machine beside him. The steady *beep beep* was replaced by something wilder and erratic.

As soon as the woman lets go of his foot, the sensation of being flogged stopped. The combined sensation of pain and pleasure stopped and the machine keeps beeping at a faster pace. She had rushed to his side, and was watching him struggle to form words with his mouth that no longer seemed to work. The noises coming from his mouth were just gargles and hisses.

She left in a hurry and somehow the presence of the fast beeping machine beside him was not an acceptable trade. Still trying to form words, he croaked for help. Where the heck was he and what was happening?

He managed to move his head a little, and look towards left and right. He was in a hospital ward of some kind and bodies on beds were to the left and right of him. Still with IV bags on stands and tubes everywhere, he was sure that he was unmoved. He tried to move his arms and found his arms free and couldn't move a little, since he was so weak.

Minutes passed, the silence was incredible except for the steady drone of the machines and the low beeping noises from all around him. The silence was replaced by the sound of footfalls. He heard hard soled shoes and squeaky rubber ones on tiled floors, walking in a hurry. A nurse in a white uniform and a man in a lab coat flapping behind were at his side. He was older, judging by the wrinkles and gray hair.

"You are awake?" the man in a lab coat asked.

He tried to say "Yes I am and where am I?" but all that came out was a series of croaks and guttural sounds. He did see a name embroidered on the lab coat stating that his name was D. Burns M.D.

He looked at John a few moments, then told the nurse to get some water and straw. He waited till she returned. He poured some room temperature water in a glass, added the straw, and held it to John's lips.

John sucked in the fluid and his mouth seemed to absorb it before the liquid got to his cheeks. The second pull on the straw was better and it got into his throat with the same effect. The third pull went down his throat and soon the dryness and tickling was gone. He pushed the straw away with his tongue and tried to speak again. This time, it came out in a whisper, but intelligible for his ears, it sounded weak and pitiful. "Where am I and how long have I been here?"

The Doctor had to lean closer to hear him. "We will get to that soon, but do you remember your name?"

John whispered his full name to the doctor, then sighed, this was going to be a memory test. Then, while he could, he rattled off his address and anything else that came to mind including his high school and college. The doctor pulled back to look at him. "And what's the last thing you remember?"

"Car, a big white SUV crossing the center line, I couldn't avoid it. I tried running my car onto the sidewalk, it happened fast, the fire, and me screaming." John managed to whisper. "What about my car?"

If you enjoyed this sample then look for **The Flog Zone.**

# MICHAEL FIORI

## Step Lovers

Taboo Erotic Romance

"Kids, we are out the door in five -- get a move on!"

The Alberts were hours away from their long-awaited and much needed vacation, and Mrs. Albert was getting nervous that she couldn't hear the rolling of her son or daughter's suitcases on the floor upstairs yet. 'It's probably Hannah making sure she has every one of her fifteen thousand bathing suits,' thought Mrs. Albert as she checked her watch and went through her carry-on in the kitchen.

A moment or two later and she could hear at least one of her children making its way down the stairs. It was Mark by the sound of it -- at around 6'2" and 200 lbs., the solid young man's steps were unmistakable. He didn't need to pack nearly as much, just a bathing suit and some warm weather clothes.

"Rio De Janeiro, here we come!" Mark exclaimed as he rounded the corner to join his mother in the kitchen. His mother thought to herself, what a handsome boy he had become, and he looked it in his sweater and jeans, though he'd obviously need to change into something warmer when they arrived.

Mark's aunt had been suckered into one of those time-share sales pitches and ended up with a few weeks in a beautiful Rio beachfront home that they couldn't make time to use. So when they offered a week to Mark's family, the four had quickly agreed to take the vacation together. Rio de Janeiro was supposed to be beautiful in February, as opposed to the cold winter winds of the Midwest.

When Mark's dad joined his wife and son in the kitchen, it was time to yell at Hannah once again, who replied:

"I'M COMING!" from Hannah upstairs, in an annoyed tone.

Hannah stopped briefly and grabbed the sexy pair of black laced panties she thought she might get to show to one of the vacationing boys she hoped to find there. Her brother would inevitably be staying out late banging some dim-witted college girls as she knew he's used to doing; why couldn't she have a little fun?

High school boys could be so frustrating. Hannah had a few times thought about giving her cherry to a boy she'd really liked, but they'd all disappointed her somehow. Whether it was bragging to their friends, or treating her badly to look cool... every one of them just wasn't worth it. But it was no wonder that they kept pursuing her -- Hannah is a stunner. She had deep green eyes with large black limbal rings around them, which looked almost animalistic when she was scolding her brother. Hannah's thick brown hair looked good straightened, as she usually wore it; or tossed up in a ponytail as it was when she headed downstairs. Her family finally saw her rounding the corner to the kitchen, wearing tight black yoga pants and an equally tight Yankees T-shirt over her 32C breasts.

"You don't even like the Yankees!" exclaimed Mark as his sister came into view. His eyes widened when he saw how little her outfit left to the imagination.

"Oh, shut up, Mark!" She got so frustrated with him sometimes. He was always picking on her, and though she sometimes liked it (it was like flirting practice for boys at school) he often got on her nerves, like now.

Mark couldn't help himself most times, she is an easy target. Plus, it helped him to distance himself in his relationship with his sister. He often felt bad how turned on he got when Hannah's friends came to visit or sleep over. As a senior in college, he wasn't supposed to find their teen bodies and their scantily clad nighttime appearances so arousing. They were his sister's age, and she was a battle herself.

Every so often, Mark thought maybe he could excuse his interest in her, hiding it behind the fact that they weren't 'technically' related. Their parents had married when both he and Hannah were very young, making them step-siblings. But they'd still grown up together, fought and played together, gone to school together... No, for all intents and purposes, Hannah was as much his sister as any of the annoying princesses, aka sisters, his buddies complained to him about. Only most of them didn't have to put up with one like his.


If you enjoyed this sample then look for **Step Lovers**.

# Less Than Yesterday

## Lilith Jones

HOT ROMANCE EROTICA

"We said we wouldn't start a baby until we'd gone for a year without needing my paycheck," she said. It hadn't been a year, had it?

"Well, I wasn't talking about starting anything tonight. It's been more than eleven months. And, if we aren't going to make the goal next month, where is the huge expenditure going to come from? . . . Not to end a sentence with a preposition or anything."

"Ted! That's not really a rule."

"Yes, dear," Ted said, sounding like he thought she was trying to change the subject. He was probably right, too, but he didn't pursue the subject. Ted was, she kept reminding herself, nice.

Thursday, a few weeks later, she started a new disk of pills. That night, with Ted working late, she realized what that meant. If she did what they had agreed, it would be her last disk of pills for a good, long while. She thought for a minute about keeping them from meeting the conditions by dipping into her savings to buy a new, costly wardrobe. The account was in her name, after all; she needn't consult Ted. Really, though, she could delay the pregnancy more sensibly than that. She could tell him that she wanted to wait longer before they had a baby.

Then, though, she would have to tell him why. Even if she trashed her savings account, he would ask why. She did not want to answer. You could tell a guy you didn't love him anymore; you couldn't tell him that you still loved him -- but you loved him less. You certainly couldn't tell him that you were afraid to have a baby with him because you were afraid that you'd love him even less in five or ten years.

And she did want babies. She had been an only child of a single mother, and she wanted four. Ted, who had been the third of four, had warned her that she was romanticizing the experience. "Sure, I want kids. We'll have one, and we can decide about the next after we have some experience with that one."

That sure didn't leave her much wiggle room now. She wanted kids; she wanted Ted's kids. They might inherit his brains, and he would be a patient father. She wanted his kids, and she wanted to raise them with him. She just wasn't sure she wanted to be with him for another eighteen years to do the job.

But, if not Ted, who? She still loved Ted. Thinking that she might someday love him so little that she might want to leave him was no reason to leave him now.

Of course, single women had children every day. So leaving Ted wasn't deciding not to ever have kids. That was stupid, though. She was afraid of having a baby now because she was afraid of raising it as a single mother. She certainly didn't want to leave Ted -- merely feared that she would want to sometime in the future.

By the time that Ted got home, she was eager to see him, so eager that she was already in a sexy nightie.

"Have dinner?" she asked.

"Yeah. I brought you some left-overs if you want them for lunch tomorrow." She carried lunch; his cafeteria was so heavily subsidized that buying lunch at work was cheaper for him than brown-bagging it. Dinner after seven was free. Nothing was too good for programmers who stayed late. "Is it too late?" For sex, he meant.

"I adore Theodore." And, really, she still did. She hadn't used that silly couplet for a while, but it still applied.

"Well, I adore Jessica, too. Give me a few minutes, and I'll prove it." While he was in the bathroom, she took off the nightie. Then she got into bed and pulled the sheet up to her neck.

Ted got into bed without baring an inch of her. Then he leaned over and kissed her before resting on one elbow and slowly drawing the sheet off her.

"It must be Christmas. Santa brought me what I've always wanted." He kissed her again. Then his mouth trailed down to her right breast. His chin scratched, but the scratches were exciting. When his tongue and lips on her nipple had aroused her, she spread her legs. He stroked her cleft until she tensed.

"Ted."

"Yes." He moved over her and between her knees, which she raised. Then he opened her, filled her. "Jess." His chest hair tickled her nipples as he moved above her and inside her. She licked salt from where his neck joined his shoulder. Her arousal gyred upward with each of his strokes. The tension broke, and she thrust herself at him and around him.

"Jess," he said as she clutched around him. "Sssi," as he drove her into the mattress. "Cah!" as he throbbed within her contractions. He collapsed on her, and they gasped into each other's ears.

Somewhat later, he pulled himself off and lay on his side inches away. When she backed into him, he wrapped himself around her.

"You are," he whispered, "the sexiest woman in the whole world." They fell asleep in the spoon, although they woke on their own sides these days. She put the nightgown on and covered it with a bathrobe before cooking breakfast. They kissed lightly before going out the door on their separate ways to their separate work.

It wasn't that Ted ignored her satisfaction, she mused on the commute. He took care to bring her to climax every time. It was just that he brought her to climax in almost the same way almost every time. Ted was a considerate lover -- just as he was considerate about doing his share of the housework and letting her choose her share of their TV shows and her share of their entertainment and socializing. Ted was nice. Was nice enough?

If you enjoyed this sample then look for **<u>Less Than Yesterday</u>**.

## WANT FREE COPIES OF MY BOOKS?

Just visit my blog and download free copies of my books:

awesomeauthors.org/justplainbob